DATE DUE		

White Wolf's Outlaw Legion

HAL DUNNING

Sagebrush
Large Print Westerns

Library of Congress Cataloging-in-Publication Data

Dunning, Hal, 1907-
    White wolf's outlaw legion
        p.   cm.
    ISBN 1-57490-406-X (lg. print : hardcover)
    1. Large type books. I. Title

    PS3507.A848 W46 2001
    813'.54—dc21   2001040419
        20.95

Cataloging in Publication Data is available from
the British Library and the National Library of Australia.

Sagebrush Large Print Westerns are published in the United
States and Canada by Thomas T. Beeler, Publisher, PO Box 659,
Hampton Falls, New Hampshire 03844-0659. ISBN 1-57490-406-X

Published in the United Kingdom, Eire, and the Republic of
South Africa by Isis Publishing Ltd, 7 Centremead, Osney
Mead, Oxford OX2 0ES England. ISBN 0-7531-6457-4

Published in Australia and New Zealand by Bolinda Publishing
Pty Ltd, 17 Mohr Street, Tullamarine, Victoria, Australia, 3043
ISBN 1-74030-314-8

Manufactured by Sheridan Books in Chelsea, Michigan.

White Wolf's
Outlaw Legion

A STRANGE INVITATION

IT WAS ON TUESDAY THAT THE "WOLF" STEPPED INTO the Last Chance Saloon and blasted the life out of "Sheeny Mike." The place was crowded with Sheeny Mike's cronies. Jim-twin Allen walked straight to Sheeny and announced that he was a mangy coyote and unfit to live. Then Allen started his count of three. At "two" Sheeny clawed desperately for his gun and died with it undrawn. Allen escaped through a hail of lead.

On the following Thursday Captain Harry Harrison of the Rangers entered the place and made his strange announcement. The saloon was crowded with booted and spurred, heavily armed riders. The air was thick with tobacco smoke and rank with the fumes of stale beer and unwashed humanity. The loud talk and blasphemous boasting died away at the entrance of the Ranger. Twenty pairs of eyes stared at him with hostile surprise.

"Gents," he asked coolly yet loudly, "will one of you tell Jim Allen that I want to see him? I'll wait at Mesquite Point from the seventh until the fifteenth."

He quietly turned his back on the crowd of desperadoes and walked from the saloon.

For a brief moment sheer astonishment held the ruffians speechless. It was "Dutch" Ogal who broke the silence with a discordant laugh. Dutch was the dead Sheeny Mike's successor.

" 'Come into my parlor, said the spider to the fly,' " he bellowed vociferously.

"Huh, that's sure got me beat. A Ranger who boasts about bein' death on long riders sendin' an invite to the

1

Wolf, the fastest gun on the border!" "Long Tom" Brady cried with an oath.

"Slim" Mason, a slender man with a pale, impassive face, fixed his cold gray eyes on the lanky rider.

"Fastest gun?" he challenged.

Long Tom Brady shrugged. "Maybe, Slim, you can sling a quicker gun. I ain't sayin' you can't. But there's sure a damn easy way to find out."

"Which will be the first time I see the Wolf. Sheeny Mike was my friend." Slim Mason's voice was cold and without expression, yet he enunciated his words as clearly as an actor.

"I'm bettin' my pile on you, Slim," Dutch Ogal admired.

"Which has nothin' to do with that Ranger's fool offer," Long Tom said with another shrug.

He had his own opinion as to what would happen if Slim ever clashed with the Wolf, but he was quite willing to change the subject, as the pale-faced killer was known to be of uncertain temper, and indisputably the best gun in that room.

"I see a copy of the *Clarion* tother day," spoke up "Kid" Riker. "There was a big piece in it roastin' the governor 'cause the Rangers couldn't clean up the border. They tole him he oughter make Allen a Ranger an' give him a free hand down here. Maybe Cap Harrison is goin' to offer the Wolf a job."

"Hell, it's this way," Dutch Ogal cried. "The Rangers is in wrong; they're bein' roasted by every one. If they could nab the Wolf, it would stop talk for a while. Cap Harrison is hopin' Allen's curiosity will make him show up. If he does, I'm bettin' a couple of dozen Rangers will open on him pronto. And I for one sure hope the Wolf shows, and afore he gets blown full of holes, cashes in a bunch of damn Rangers."

This about summed up the opinion and the desires of most of those present. But there was one man who held a different view. "Silent Sam" Henry was a friend of Jim Allen. He had about the same build and was about the same age as Slim Mason. But whereas Slim was pale and dark-haired, Silent was tow-headed, and his face was tanned to the color of leather.

His open, unblinking blue eyes were reckless rather than hard, and his firmly closed mouth was sardonic rather than evil. By nature he was noncommunicative, and his name, "Silent," was well-earned.

He would have welcomed a chance to have it out with Slim Mason, but Mason was the foreman of the Frying Pan, and seven of his outfit were with him. Silent Sam was not foolhardy. So he wisely decided to postpone the issue with Slim for a more propitious moment. He finished his drink, then leisurely strolled outside. He swung into his saddle and slowly trotted from town.

Four Point Crossing was an unsavory place, an outlaw capital. There was no law there except that of the gang—crooked politicians and outlaws, who bossed Cactus County.

Silent Sam's mouth drew down in distaste. He cursed the fate that condemned him to live in such places. There was a gallows waiting in some State for every man back there. Even Kid Riker, not yet nineteen and the youngest of the crew, was wanted in Montana for a cowardly murder. Yet the unsavory gang who ruled the county moved about freely and snapped their fingers at any sheriff who attempted to serve a warrant. This immunity accounted for Silent Sam's presence there. He was wanted for a killing in self-defense, that had been

3

marked as murder in the courthouse records of his home town. Would he ever have a chance to start a new life, to live with decent people again?

He made a grimace and shook his head. There was no turning back once a man started down the long trail.

It was long past nightfall when Silent Sam reached Pineville, his destination. He dropped off his weary horse, turned him over to a hostler to be grained and watered, then entered the Golden Buck Saloon.

Here he found the same type of hard-eyed riders. As he swung open the door every man grew tense and shot an alert glance at him, then, recognizing him, relaxed. Several men called him by name and shouted a boisterous invitation to join them at the bar.

He was startled to find that Captain Harrison had also been there, and the riders were speculating in much loud talk as to the meaning of the Ranger's message. Silent Sam caught the same hatred of Allen that he had heard at Sheeny Mike's.

He listened to the excited comments while he dined on sardines, cheese and beer. Then he saddled his horse and continued on his way.

Sam was both perplexed and disturbed at the Ranger's message. It was hardly possible that the Ranger's invitations to the Wolf was of the nature of a social call—it must be a trap. Captain Harrison was noted all through the State for his uncompromising attitude toward outlaws. He was an old-timer, and held to the grim axiom that a dead outlaw saved the State the cost of a trial.

Silent Sam determined to visit "Silver" Conklin, who was an old friend of Allen and had known him since he was a boy. Silent grinned happily, but a second later an inner voice brought a flush to his cheek.

"You ain't ridin' all night just to see Silver and ask him about Allen. You got another visit in your mind," the voice jeered.

Silent rode through the night with only the stars as his companions. The trail dropped from Skeleton Pass over the divide into Bedford County. That neighboring county was also held—though more loosely—by the same lawless band which controlled Cactus.

The stars slowly paled. Then the sun shot above the divide and drenched the rolling valley with golden light. The trail dipped around a bend, and there, before him, lay a broad street, shaded by tall trees. It was Sunset City.

The houses were well-built, clean and tidy, surrounded by flower and vegetable gardens. Silent got a shave and bought a new shirt. Then he led his horse up the street to an adobe house, surrounded by a wall. His eyes sparkled with pleasurable anticipation as he turned in the gate and glanced about.

The courtyard was a riot of color, and bees hummed among the flowers. Grapevines, heavy with purple fruit, were trained against the wall. The house was long, low and rambling.

Silent hitched his horse to a post, walked down a covered gallery, and turned into a huge, low-ceilinged room. It was gay with bright Navajo blankets, painted wicker chairs, and low tables aglow with shaded lamps.

" 'Lo, Silent. Now we'll be talked to death," cried a young, cheerful voice.

Silent swung about and swept off his hat. A girl with a tray stood in the doorway at the opposite side of the room. She was slender, golden-haired, bright-eyed, and her face was alight with mischievous amusement.

" 'Lo, Stella," Silent answered shortly.

5

His greeting was abrupt, but his eyes were eloquent, and proclaimed their message so directly that color flooded the girl's cheeks.

"Is this a business or a social visit?" the girl asked quickly to hide her confusion.

"I'm starvin', an'—"

"It's business then," the girl interrupted demurely. "If you'll be seated I'll take your order in a minute."

Carrying her tray, she swept across the room to a man seated at a low table close to the open window. The light left Silent's eyes, and a frown flickered across his face. "Laughing Ed" Cummins was no friend of his. There had been bad blood between them before they both had started to haunt Casa Modoc.

Laughing Ed Cummins was a giant of a man. He weighed over two hundred, and was close to six feet four. He had the coloring and carriage of an ancient viking. He had bold blue eyes and curly yellow hair, in strong contrast to his bronzed skin. He had won his name from his laugh, which was loud and pleasant, but curiously enough held little real mirth.

He and Silent would have tangled long since except that they knew it would mean banishment for them both. Silver Conklin, Stella's father, made it a rule to eject both parties in a fight and to forbid either ever to return.

Laughing Ed saw Silent glaring at him; he threw back his head, and his lusty "Ho-ho-ho!" made the rafters ring.

Silent ignored him. He unbuckled his belt and gun and hung them on a peg by the door, then chose a table and sat with his back turned conspicuously to Laughing Ed.

Stella took his order and departed. The room began to fill with hungry customers—long riders, drifting cow-

6

punchers, travelers, and the single men of the village. Many men entered, but never a woman. Silent cursed to himself. Damn fools, making the girl suffer for the sins of her father!

His eyes followed her about the room. Her face should have been sad, but was alive with the joy of living. Her eyes should have been wistful and hurt, but were mirthful and proud.

Silver Conklin was famous all over the West as the leader of the most notorious gang of bandits since the days of Jesse James. They had robbed trains and banks and terrorized three States until at last his gang were cornered in the Pan Handle and wiped out.

Silver had been the only one to escape that bloody and famous fight. Six deputy sheriffs, five Rangers, and four of Silver's band had died that day. Silver had managed to escape, but later had been caught and put on trial. He had been acquitted, for it was impossible to find a single witness who dared to connect him with any of the robberies or holdups.

After his gang had been wiped out, Silver turned over a new leaf and attempted to bury his past. But people refused to forget, and avenged themselves by ostracizing Stella.

Gradually the men drifted outside, until Silent Sam and Laughing Ed were the only two left. The girl was first amused, then alarmed by the expressions on their faces. There was danger in the air, and the girl recognized it. She racked her woman's wits to discover a way to ease one or the other out without starting an explosion.

Laughing Ed noticed the anxiety in her eyes, and he threw back his head and laughed until the cups and plates danced on the tables. Silent's tow-colored hair bristled like a dog's hackles. He sensed that that laugh held a sneer and a challenge.

"Ho-ho!" bellowed Laughing Ed. "He hung up his gun careful-like—so there wouldn't be powder burned."

Silent swung about in his chair, and his words were as cold and evenly spaced as drops from an icicle.

"But I'll be wearin' it again when I pass the gate outside," he said.

The girl cried out. Silent was startled at the stricken fear he saw in her eyes. Then something struck him with the force of a blow. She was afraid that he would kill that laughing hyena. Never for a moment did he suspect that her fear might be for him. Before Laughing Ed could frame a reply to Silent's challenge, Silver Conklin took a hand in the affair.

"That will be all of that. One more word and you both go out—and you won't come back," he said crisply.

Silver Conklin was a tall, spare man of sixty, with silvery-white hair. His thin face was impassive, his clear blue eyes calm. Yet his quiet voice held a world of authority. Here was a leader of men, one who was used to having his orders obeyed. Instantly the two men became meek and abashed as schoolboys, lapsed into sullen silence.

"Silent, I want to see you," Silver said.

Silent glowered at Laughing Ed, then followed Silver into a small adjoining room.

"Silent, you've got to hunt up Jim Allen. Cap Harrison was here day before yesterday and left a message for him," Silver said, and then he repeated the message verbatim.

"He left the same message in Four Point and Pineville," Silent remarked.

"An' Sharon, Cactus, Casa Grandes and San Miguel," Silent said soberly.

8

"Them places, too? Huh, he sure covered all the bad towns in the three counties, didn't he? He must be plumb anxious to see Jim Allen. What do you suppose it means?" Silent spoke with unexpected loquacity.

"Don't know. But somethin's up, so you got to hit the breeze and find Jim. It's up to him to decide what he's goin' to do."

Silent nodded. "I'll find him."

Silver Conklin looked directly at Silent and said distinctly:

"An' don't come back here no more!"

"What?" Silent gasped.

Then his heart became like lead. All life went from his face as he stared blindly at the floor.

"I savvy what you mean," he said gloomily.

"Kid, don't get me wrong," Silver said with gruff kindliness. "It's only because you're a long rider I'm askin' you to stay away."

"But so is Laughin' Ed," Silent protested.

"Yeah, but he don't count, an' you do. My gal's eyes get too damn shiny when she sees you. Folks won't speak to her because her dad was Silver Conklin, the boss of the Black Riders. Next year I'm takin' her to a new country, where she'll meet decent men. I would kill her before I'd let her marry an outlaw. So, kid, you stay away."

For a long moment Silent simply stared at Silver. His face flushed, then turned deadly pale. He felt a fierce exultation at the thought that the girl cared. But he—an outlaw with a price on his head—could bring her no happiness—only grief and despair.

"Silent, I'd be glad to see you if you could ever come with a clean name," Silver said five minutes later as Silent swung into his saddle.

9

"Thanks, but there ain't no turnin' back once you start down the long trail," Silent said with bitter regret.

"Watch your back, Silent. I've known gents to laugh and laugh loud as they potted someone through the back," Silver warned. "So watch yourself. Laughin' Ed pulled out a few minutes ago."

This warning brought no dismay to Silent. If anything, he hoped that Laughing Ed would try and dry-gulch him, for the killing of that man might ease the ache in his heart.

He nodded to Silver, then trotted through the gate and took the trail south toward the desert, where he hoped to find Jim Allen and deliver Captain Harrison's strange message.

A RANGER RECRUIT

A WEEK AFTER THE RANGER HAD LEFT HIS MESSAGE AT Sheeny Mike's and the other outlaw strongholds, three men sat in a large tent on the tip of Mesquite Point. Captain Harry Harrison was a grizzled man of over fifty. Faded blue eyes looked out from a face that was tanned and so hard that it might have been carved from granite.

He was an old-timer, and had been a member of the Rangers for years. He had discarded his boots, his guns and his coat, and sat cocked back in his chair in his undershirt, his stockinged feet on the table.

His brother, Governor "Big Bill" Harrison, sat next to him at the table, studying a pile of reports and maps. The governor was younger than his fighting brother. He was a big, genial-looking man, dressed in a frock coat and string tie. His black slouch hat was pushed back on his head. At first sight he looked the typical politician, but his eyes were steady, honest, and direct, and he was as capable of putting up a fight as his hard-faced brother.

Amos Stringer, the third man, was the State's attorney general. He was a thin, stoop-shouldered, nervous man of forty-five. His eyes were small, keen, and never still. They looked from beneath a bulging, bold forehead. He was pacing nervously up and down the tent with his hands clasped behind his back.

"Of all the fool things!" he snapped. "The governor of a great State, its attorney general and one of its chief police officers, cooling their heels in this wilderness to await the pleasure of a notorious outlaw! I tell you, Bill, this is a mad idea of yours."

The governor looked at him with amusement, and his florid face lighted with a slow smile.

"Amos, stop fussing. Can't you forget Allen and just imagine that you are on a vacation? Remember the trout. You can't deny that the fishing is good," he said in a sonorous voice.

"Yes, the fishing is good," Amos Stringer admitted. He took two or three more quick turns up and down the tent, then added querulously:

"But we don't even know if he's coming."

"He'll come," the Ranger captain grunted.

"You didn't promise him a safe conduct. I can't understand why you think he'll take the chance of thrusting his head into a noose," Stringer said irritably.

"You've had your nose in law books all your life. You don't savvy gents like the Wolf and me," the captain drawled good-naturedly. "Suppose I had promised him a safe conduct. He would have had to trust my word, wouldn't he? Now I told him I wanted to

11

see him—just that and no more. He knows me, and savvys that means he's free to come and go. If the Wolf was warp-brained and crooked, like most outlaws, he would figure I was also crooked, and think this was a trap. But he ain't crooked. His word is as good as mine, so he'll trust me."

"Maybe so," Amos Stringer admitted grudgingly. "But the Rangers have come to a pretty pass when they have to seek recruits from the ranks of the outlaws."

"I was once proud of this uniform, but now I'm gettin' ashamed of it. It's getting to mean the badge of grafters and cowards. Unless things improve quick, I hope you'll disband the Rangers before their old reputation is completely ruined," the captain growled.

"The Rangers are sick and need a desperate remedy. That's why I agreed to Sam Hogg's suggestion of enlisting Allen," the governor sighed.

"What does he look like, this Allen?" Stringer demanded.

"I never saw him, but he's small and no-account-lookin', from what I hear," the captain replied.

"Blendine's *Clarion* and his crowd of grafters will raise a howl when they learn you're filling the Rangers with outlaws," Stringer said nervously.

"I have a precedent. Governor Miller did it in the late '80s. The Mayor of El Paso did it when he appointed Doc Candee town marshal. Besides, I'm only doin' what my opponents told me to do. They have been nagging me in a dozen papers to make Allen a Ranger and to give him a free hand to clean up this mess along the border."

"An' Ed Blendine, the darned hypocrite, is back of the whole grafting gang who are ruining these three counties," Stringer flared. "He tol' you to appoint Allen just to get you in a hole. He and—"

Captain Harry Harrison held up his hand for silence. His head was cocked, and his eyes were fixed on the tent flap. The other two stared questioningly at him.

"The Wolf's here," he said softly.

The governor swung about and stared at the opening. His eyes sparkled with excitement and curiosity. He felt the thrill of a small boy waiting for the sight of his first circus parade.

They heard Corporal Pat Tait speak gruffly outside:

" 'Lo, Jim. Knew you would come. Nope, keep your guns. This is a gent's game. They're waitin' in the tent for you."

There came a short laugh in reply, the soft crunching of feet in sand, and then silence. The three men held their breaths as they waited. The tent flap flipped back, and two men slipped in. The three men fixed their eyes on the one who entered first, wasting only a single glance on the second.

So that was the famous Wolf! Nothing very frightening about him. He was of medium height and slender, with a rather hard face and watchful eyes. His hands hung loosely near the butts of his guns. He stood on his toes, alert and suspicious, as a cat with a strange dog.

His companion was even smaller than he—a veritable runt in size, dressed in a flannel shirt and jeans so faded, patched, and tattered that they would have been spurned by even the most miserable hobo. It is doubtful if any of the three even noticed his crossed belts and the two big guns tied down in professional gunman style.

His strange eyes were alight with amusement. His big, loose mouth was split in a good-natured grin which extended from ear to ear. This grin became even wider when he saw that the three men ignored him and

13

concentrated their attention on Silent Sam Henry. While Silent was nervous and uneasy, Jim Allen himself was as relaxed and as much at ease as a well-fed puppy.

Captain Harry Harrison cleared his throat and said to Silent:

"I take it you're Jim Allen. I'm thankin' you for for comin'. I reckon you know the governor, by his looks, anyway." He nodded at his brother, then jerked his thumb at Stringer. "He's the attorney general. He'll tell you what we want."

Amos Stringer had recovered his wits. He felt disappointed and cheated. Somehow he felt that the notorious Wolf's looks belied his reputation. He stared at Silent and shook his head.

He briefly sketched the rise of the crooked political machine which, starting in Cactus County, had already spread to Bedford and Sharon, the two adjoining counties. He said that things had reached such a pass that the voters dared not call their souls their own. It was impossible to find any one to run in opposition to the machine's candidates.

The prosecuting attorneys, the sheriffs, and even the judges in the three counties were all members of the gang. The gang could rob and commit murder without danger of prosecution. Honest business men were being ruined. Cattlemen were losing stock, and dared not raise a hand in protest. The gang had made an example of "Old Man" Summers. He had caught rustlers at work and had summarily hanged the men. Summers had been arrested and tried for murder. Perjured witnesses had sworn that Summers had hung the two men to even an old grudge. He had been convicted—the jury dared not acquit him.

Summer's lawyer had appealed the case, and the superior court would undoubtedly grant a new trial. But while the cattleman had been in jail, his range had been swept clean of cattle, so that now he was completely ruined.

"Gentlemen, the county officers are corrupt," Stringer continued earnestly. "The governor dispatched Rangers to keep order, but they also failed."

"The old-timers were murdered, shot at from ambush. The new type, mamma-boy Rangers, were either bribed or intimidated," Captain Harrison growled. "A Ranger was once respected—now he's laughed at!"

"Allen, I'm putting it up to you," the governor cut in bluntly. "You can take a couple of friends with you. I'll give you and them free pardons for all you have done in this State if you'll clean up these counties for me."

"A pardon?" Silent cried.

"A pardon that will wash you as white as snow," the governor said.

The look of a condemned man who has just received a reprieve leaped into Silent's eyes. He recalled Silver Conklin's last words. He would be welcome when his slate was clean. His eyes were shining with hope as he swung about and looked at his friend.

"Jim," he cried eagerly, "you'll do it—an' take me in on it?"

"Jim—Jim Allen?" the three exclaimed together.

They switched their eyes from Silent to the ragged, freckle-faced boy. That kid the Wolf? Impossible!

It was hard enough to think of Silent as that notorious killer—but that grinning, puny runt! It was farcical! The thought entered the governor's mind that he was being played with, and he frowned. But the corporal had greeted one of these two as the Wolf. One glance at Silent's face convinced him of the truth. He was staring at Allen as if he were his savior.

15

"You're Jim Allen?" the Ranger captain asked foolishly.

"Yeah, I'm him," Allen replied.

The grin faded from Allen's face as he looked at Silent.

"Silent, I'm sorry, but she can't be did," he said softly.

The three men were both perplexed and confounded at the unexpected turn of affairs. They looked in amazement at Allen's face, which seemed to have aged a thousand years. It was as wrinkled as old parchment, and his eyes held the hopeless sadness of the ages.

"You mean you refuse?" Stringer cried irritably. "Damn you, you got to, or I'll have you arrested!"

"Like hell you will!" the Ranger snapped.

"Look here, Allen, you'll get a free pardon, and I'll even try to get you pardoned by other States," the governor promised.

"I'm sorry."

"We might arrange a cash bonus," Stringer suggested.

Allen made no reply.

Captain Harrison then spoke:

"Allen, you savvy that forty thousand folks are being ruined by a couple of hundred crooked politicians and thugs?"

Allen nodded.

"You know they've just voted a bill changin' the county seat from Carson to Four Point Crossing? Which means real estate will go down in Carson and go up in Four Point. Every bit of land about the Crossing is owned by a syndicate. It's the biggest steal the State has ever known."

"Are you going to let a few dirty outlaws ruin decent men and women?" Stringer demanded heatedly.

16

"Ain't you forgettin' I'm an outlaw?" Allen countered simply.

"Shut up, Amos!" the Ranger snapped. Then he faced Allen again. "Meanin' you've been runnin' on the outlaw side of the fence for so long that you, would feel a traitor if you turned against them just because they are outlaws?"

"Somethin' like that."

The Ranger's face was sparkling with triumph as he asked:

"Allen, why did you down Sheeny Mike?"

" 'Cause he was a skunk."

"Was it because he ruined that Mexican gal who killed herself?" the Ranger demanded.

"Yeah—a Mex gal is a gal just the same."

The captain's eyes were shining with excitement as he leaped to his feet and started to rummage among the papers on his desk. Silent watched him with renewed hope. The captain thrust a clipping at Allen.

"Read that!" he said.

Allen read the slip slowly. When he looked up his face had again changed. It still looked old, but it had an impersonal savagery about it. Little flecks of yellow shone deep down in his eyes.

"You mean this gang stole that feller's gal and wife just because he dared run for sheriff against one of their men?" he asked flatly.

"Just that. No one has heard of them since. I'm hopin' they was murdered and not sent across the border," the Ranger said grimly.

The Ranger picked up a sheaf of letters.

"These letters, Allen, are all from people in Cactus County, asking protection for their womenfolks. They say a gal ain't safe in that country any more. No woman dares

17

leave the house for fear she'll be insulted. Three gals and an old woman have been murdered by those beasts."

He tossed the package back on the table and picked up a letter. "This letter is addressed to the governor. It's from the head of the Federal narcotic squad. It says the whole of America is being flooded with dope, run across the border into one of those three counties. The Federal agents are hampered, spied on. Three have been arrested on a trumped-up charge, and two murdered.

"There's no doubt that Blendine is the head of a big dope ring. He is using the chaos which he has deliberately created in Cactus and the other counties to run in dope from Mexico," the governor added.

Then both he and the Ranger gloried in the expression that had leaped into Allen's eyes. His eyes were those of a wolf now—yellow and savage with fire.

"The damned skunks!" Allen said flatly.

Silent leaped to his feet, and his face was shining. The two brothers knew that they had succeeded.

"Allen, we play the game this way. We arrest you for murder—you are then freed on bail. After that you will be free to go any place within the State. Not even the national authorities can arrest you or extradite you until you have been tried and have paid your debt to this sovereign State."

In a flash the light faded from Allen's eyes. He was once more as happy and amused as a kid about to play a practical joke.

"That works?" he asked the attorney general.

Amos Stringer nodded.

"An' I can play the game my way? Meanin' I'm not expected to slap every gent in jail just because he has a record. An' I can collect a few gents who I can trust to help out?" Allen asked.

"You can both deal the cards and play 'em to suit yourself. You can name the devil himself and I'll make him a Ranger," the governor promised.

Allen grinned at Silent. "I'm appointing you now."

"Poor devil," the governor muttered as he saw the expression in Silent's eyes. He added aloud to Allen:

"Here's your commission as captain. Now, what are you goin' to do first?"

"Send out a call for a few other lone wolves. Gather 'em in a pack. Then set 'em on the trail." He was quiet for a moment, then he wrote some names on two slips of paper. He handed them to the Ranger. "One is a list of long riders, tother is gents in the service who are my friends. You send orders to have 'em meet me at Sunset City."

"It's done. Then what?"

"Didn't you say these hombres has just switched the county seat?"

"Yes, but Four Point is also the headquarters of the gang."

"Huh, if you're aimin' to smash a hornets' nest, the thing to do is to walk right up and hit her hard with a flat board."

"Sure, but you'll get stung."

"The gents what will be with me know how to sting themselves. If you knock the nest loose from the branch, the hornets raise hell, but their nest is sure gone." He stopped and grinned boyishly. "Four Corners is the outlaw capital. So we'll make her the headquarters of the outlaw legion!"

Then he swung about, followed by Silent, who moved like a man in a dream, and left the tent. The other three were silent for a moment, then the governor grinned wryly.

19

"I think he'll do it," he said.

"Sure. I got an idea there won't be much law, but a hell of a lot of justice the way he does it," the Ranger spoke grimly.

THE OUTLAW LEGION

FIVE DAYS AFTER THAT STRANGE MEETING BETWEEN the governor of a great State and the most famous outlaw of all time, the *Star*, the government's mouthpiece, gave a carefully deleted account of that interview.

The rival paper, the *Clarion*, owned by Ed Blendine, the governor's bitter political rival, treated the whole thing as a joke. The people read both papers, laughed and dismissed the thing from their minds.

The following week the storm broke. Jim Allen was arrested for murder, duly committed before judge Guttenburg, and released on bail. The same day the *Star* carried a notice of his appointment as a captain in the State Rangers.

The *Clarion* came out with huge headlines and a fierce attack. It printed the wildest gossip about Allen and assailed the governor for having appointed to the Rangers a man who was wanted for murder in a dozen States.

The *Star* coolly reminded its rival paper that as Allen had never been convicted of any crime, they were laying themselves open to a libel suit in calling him a murderer. The governor smilingly told the interviewers that he had simply followed the advice of his political opponents and that they should be the last ones to complain.

The whole affair appealed to the voters' sense of humor, and many thought it was a shrewd move on the governor's part. He had appointed a notorious outlaw to smash a nest of thieves and murderers. Let Allen's outlaw legion kill and be killed!

The residents of Sunset City were agog with excitement when it became known that Jim Allen was visiting Silver Conklin. Stella Conklin's cheeks were flushed with joy

Silent Sam was a pleasing sight in his neat gray uniform, but Stella had successfully taken the conceit out of him and reduced him to a state of bewilderment and doubt. The restaurant was crowded, not only by villagers, but by hard-faced riders, all curious to see the famous Wolf. But they were disappointed, for Allen did not appear.

It was Long Tom Brady who announced the news to his cronies in Sheeny Mike's place. The outlaws were momentarily stunned.

"The Wolf a Ranger! That sure gives him a hard hand to beat," Kid Riker exclaimed.

Cyrus C. Thompson was the political boss of Cactus County. In the days when he had ridden the long trail, he had been a husky youngster, but years of prosperity and soft living had turned his muscles into rolls of fat. His unblinking, fishlike eyes were almost hidden by wrinkles of fat. A great diamond sparkled on his pudgy hand as he thumped the bar and glared at Kid Riker.

"The Wolf may be a Ranger, but my offer for his pelt goes," he shouted. "And don't forget that the man who downs him will be tried right here in Four Point, which is now the county seat."

❖❖❖

21

It was on account of that speech that heavily armed riders haunted Silver's restaurant. While they ate, they balanced their naked guns on their knees beneath the table. But Allen did not show himself. As the days slipped by and he did not appear, both the outlaws and the citizens decided that the whole thing was a fake.

The citizens of Sunset City refused to get excited even when Corporal Pat Tait, followed by three Rangers, rode into town and dismounted before the Casa Modoc. They had seen many Rangers during the past two years, and no longer respected them.

But when two strange riders jogged down the street one sunlit afternoon, the town began to buzz with excitement.

"I knows those fellers. I see their picture in the paper, They're the Yuma Kid and Pete Borden. They're always together, and they're the fastest gunmen in New Mexico," the man stuttered.

One was a bright-faced, pleasant-looking boy with curly hair and prominent teeth. The other, a few years older, was of medium height and dark. Their eyes were bright and hard when they stopped before Casa Modoc.

"There comes another," a second villager pointed along the eastern trail. "Gosh dang, that's Doc Candee, the killer outlaw and Texas sheriff!"

"There come the Cole brothers—they're both wanted bad in Kansas," an old prospector shrilled. "They use rifles just like they was short guns."

One by one the gunmen vanished into the courtyard, and the villagers gathered in an awe-struck circle about the entrance. Toward sundown three more riders drifted into town, slouched down in their saddles.

"Bad Bill Rogers, the Colorado marshal; Pat Garrett, the Arizona sheriff; and Dude Malone, gambler and killer," the crowd murmured as they recognized the famous gunmen.

"Hell's goin' to pop," the old prospector muttered.

The wolves were gathering—answering the call of the pack.

Men of blood, killers all, the pick of all the gunmen west of the Mississippi, they had answered the call of their king—ridden far and fast, to answer the blood call. Each man there owed a debt to Allen, and had journeyed far to pay it.

" 'Lo, Yuma. We sorta met like this afore," "Bad Bill" cried.

"Yeah, that time up in Colorado. We didn't need our guns that time, but I reckon we'll smell smoke hereabouts," Yuma retorted cheerfully. "The Wolf saved my neck once, but after this time I figure he'll be paid in full."

"Yeah, that's the way I feel. A bunch of bad hombres had me cornered once, and he butted in and pulled me free," Bad Bill explained.

Corporal Pat Tait glanced around the room at the outlaws and sheriffs, and whispered to his group of Rangers:

"With those fellers in uniform and back of me, I'd clean out hell and the devil himself!"

"I'm dang glad they're on our side," young Bob Carver replied fervently.

Then Jim Allen entered the room. He always looked ridiculously boyish, but now, dressed in uniform, he looked even more so. Even his crossed belts and low-hung guns failed to make him look anything but a masquerading boy.

When the group of hard-faced gunmen saw him they

23

first stared, then laughed in sheer wonder and joy.

"Gosh, Jim, if a truant officer ever saw you he would turn you over his knee and give you a good lickin' for playin' hooky," Doc Candee chortled.

"Jim, you always was runt-sized, but them duds make you look no bigger than a peanut," the Yuma Kid cried boisterously.

"Huh, you big-toothed galoot, laugh your fool head off and see if you can make me feel bad. Clothes like these is waitin' for you-all. But first I want to tell you how things are fixed, and any gent who doesn't want to ride with me can hit the breeze an' no hard feelin'," Allen said with a grin.

He explained briefly what he intended to do.

"Meanin', we don't touch no long rider unless he's a skunk to boot?" Yuma Kid asked.

"Yep; unless he's mixed up with dope runnin', hurtin' gals, or other devil tricks, he goes scot-free," Allen assured them. "An' me an' you fellers is to decide. We deal the cards an' play the hands."

"Then I'm with you," Yuma stated decisively.

"Me, too," the others chorused.

It was a strange sight to see those grim-faced men disporting themselves like so many schoolboys as they donned their new uniforms and hurled jibes at each other.

Just when they had fastened the last buttons, buckled their belts about their waists and patted their guns into place, Kid Riker and four companions chose that moment to appear. He and his friends had left Pineville and sworn never to return without the Wolf's ears.

They had been drinking on their trip to Sunset City, and were full of false courage as they swaggered into the restaurant. They bristled like so many mangy curs

24

when they sighted Corporal Tait and his three Rangers. The corporal ignored them.

"I never did tucker to Rangers. Always figured a Ranger to be a half brother to a horned toad. But the old crop had some guts, which is more than the present bunch has," one of them shouted.

"Where's this here Wolf? I aim to clip his ears," Kid Riker hiccupped. His face was mottled, sweating, inflamed with drink.

It was at that moment that Allen, followed by his outlaw legion, filed into the room. Kid Riker leaped to his feet and advanced a few paces to meet them. He planted his feet well apart to steady himself. He had reached the stage when drink robbed him of all discretion.

"If you wasn't backed by a bunch of sissies, I'd curry your comb, you snake!" Kid Riker shouted.

"Kid, take a good look at the fellers' faces back of me. Maybe you don't know 'em all, but you sure know some. Take a look, then pull in your horns," Allen advised.

"To hell with 'em! Tell 'em to keep out of this or I'll blow you apart. Or maybe you're goin' to hide behind that lousy uniform?" Kid snarled. His talonlike hand hovered over the butt of his gun.

Even if Kid Riker chose to disregard Allen's warning, his backers had no such idea. They took one swift glance along the row of faces back of Allen and gasped. Their belligerency left them, and they collapsed like punctured balloons.

If strictly sober, all four would have discreetly avoided pitting themselves against Allen alone. Now, seeing him backed by all those men, their faces blanched, and their souls quaked.

25

"Kid, behave!" one cried hastily.

When Kid Riker continued to glower at Allen, the man added:

"Gents, we ain't in this."

The four backed away and half raised their hands. This defection of his friends only made Kid Riker more determined to force a show-down with Allen.

"You're hidin' behind them," he shouted.

"Shucks, Kid, I don't want to kill you. When you sober up and they tell you what you said you'll die of fright," Allen said good-naturedly.

Allen's hand made a blurred streak as the last words left his lips. The Kid's hands closed on the butt of his gun, and he uttered a howl of pain and rage as Allen rapped him across the knuckles with the barrel of his Colt.

"Shucks, Kid, who ever tole you that you was a gunman?" Allen cried. "Now put 'em up and be good."

Kid Riker backed away, nursing his bruised knuckles. The pain of his broken hand drove the fumes of alcohol from his befuddled brain and brought back his sanity. His face paled, perspiration gathered in drops on his forehead, and he reached for the sky with ludicrous haste.

"Corporal, take their guns and then chain 'em together," Allen ordered in a determined voice.

The five riders were disarmed, chained together and herded into a storeroom at the back.

"Saddle up, gents. We're goin' to twist the tiger's tail," Allen announced cheerfully.

"Jim, come here," Silver Conklin called.

Allen followed the white-haired ex-outlaw into his private room. The old man seemed to be at a loss for words. He stared at the floor while Allen waited in silence. Then his head came up and he squared his shoulders. He pointed to a sword hanging over the fireplace.

"Jim, that was my dad's sword. It was given him for somethin' he done in the reb's army. He went all through that war. He—he was respected when he died. Jim, I want you to sign me up in the Rangers," Silver said slowly.

"Sure, Silver, but I want you to realize she's dangerous."

"Not with that mob you got out there."

"I reckon they're the best bunch of gun slingers in the States, but we're outnumbered bad. An' those fellers will hit us secret, for we don't know who we're fightin' yet."

"Yeah, maybe so," Silver Conklin smiled. "You tryin' to scare me?"

"Nope, that can't be did. But I was thinkin' of your gal."

"I've took steps to have her taken care of. Jim, where're you goin' tonight?"

"Four Point Crossing is the county seat now. So it ought to be Ranger headquarters," Allen replied readily.

Silver made a rapid calculation, then said:

"You got nine amateur Rangers and four regular ones. With you that makes fourteen."

"Yeah, but don't forget that me and those nine amateurs each pack two guns, which makes us count twenty," Allen said.

"Cyrus Thompson—for he's the gent you're up against—has about forty. Then most of the townsfolk will throw in with him. You're doin' right to surprise 'em afore they know your gang is about, but you're goin' against tough odds."

27

"Sure," Allen admitted.

"Jim, I want to ride with you," Silver said earnestly. "You never knew it, but, Jim, afore I went bad as a kid I was a Ranger, an' I would sorta like to pay some of the debt I owe by dyin' one."

"Get your hoss, Silver," Allen said simply. "We're ridin' pronto."

FIRST BLOOD

ALLEN KNEW THAT HIS JOB WOULD BE A DANGEROUS one. Thompson and his lieutenants, Dutch Ogal's gunmen, would fight. There was no doubt of that. The hangers-on would harass his flanks like a lot of cowardly coyotes. Once the resistance of the gunmen was broken, the rest would take to their holes like rats. But until then, the town ruffians might prove to be annoying, even turning the tide of battle.

Covered wagons with supplies and an escort of an officer and three more Rangers were waiting for him a short distance from town. That would give him four more men, and possibly the wagoners could be tempted to throw in with him.

It was close to midnight when they reached Pineville. Allen sent his men through the town in pairs, and all managed to slip through without being seen. They rode steadily and hard all that night.

At dawn Allen called a halt for a short rest. While the men were drinking scalding-hot coffee, he explained his plans. He divided his force and placed one group under Pat Garrett and the other under Bad Bill Rogers.

Garrett was to enter the town from the south, while Bad Bill's force was to come from the north. Each group was to head for Sheeny Mike's place, to take and hold it at all cost.

The saloon was an old trading post, and had been built when the Comanches raided along the trail named for them. It was a large, square building with a courtyard in the center. It stood on a corner, and whoever held it, held the town, for it was a veritable fortress.

"Jim, excuse me for buttin' in," Corporal Tait said apologetically, "but I figure you ought to warn the boys to hold their fire until fired on. Otherwise there'll be hell to pay. The papers will raise a howl."

"Shucks," Allen snorted, "we could let 'em shoot a dozen times and we would be blamed for startin' it just the same. So, boys, don't go off half-cocked, but if you see a gent gettin' set to shoot, let him have it first, and shoot to kill."

"That's sense, but it ain't regulations," Corporal Tait confided to a fellow Ranger.

"Yeah, he's a wolf, but he ain't no trained one," the Ranger grinned.

Silent Sam objected strenuously when Allen picked him and Silver Conklin to accompany him in search of the supply wagons.

"Look-a here, Jim, just because we're friends it ain't fair for you to go savin' me an' keepin' me out of the fun," he protested. "I got to have my chance to do somethin'."

Silver Conklin smiled to himself. Silent was showing up well, but now he was proving that he had more nerve than discrimination.

When Allen finally located his supply wagons, he received a reinforcement which was as important as it was unexpected. The wagons were camped on the top of a rocky knoll, a short distance from the Crawling Creek Trail. He rode up, slipped from the back of his gray, and glanced about.

" 'Lo, Jim," Lieutenant O'Brien greeted. "It's three years since you made me hang on my ears while you downed that skunk."

" 'Lo, Tim; darn you, but I'm plum' glad they sent you," Allen cried delightedly as he shook hands.

Three Rangers crowded about them as they talked. Allen briefly explained his plans.

"Who's the masquerading kid?" a jeering voice demanded.

Jim Allen swung about and saw a heavily whiskered man, dressed in a frock coat, extra high-heeled boots, and high-crowned hat, wearing two low-hung guns. For a moment he was too taken aback to speak. Then a slow smile started and continued until it looked about to disrupt his face. Allen pointed at the little whiskered man and addressed the lieutenant.

"Who's the runt on stilts what is tryin' to make himself man-sized?" he asked sarcastically.

The Rangers grinned, and three men who stepped from the shelter of a wagon sent them an answering grin and waited. Silver and Silent swung from their horses and joined the circle.

"If you don't put a halter on that fool grin, the top of your head will fall off," Jack Allen warned with pretended seriousness.

"Why, hello, Jack! What did that wife of yours do to you—kick you out? What you want me to do—go see her and fix it up for you?" Jim asked, and his grin became even wider. "You remember, it was me who proposed for you."

The three men by the wagon howled. Jim and Jack

Allen were twins. Rose, Jack's wife, had found it impossible to tell them apart when they were both clean-shaven. Jack had been tardy in proposing, so Jim had helped him out. Jack awoke one day and discovered he was engaged. What the three men were laughing about was that it was Jim who had received the first engagement kiss, and he had maliciously told Jack about it.

"You stay away from Rose. If you pull that trick again, I'll sure bust you proper," Jack threatened, half in earnest.

Then the two brothers shook hands. They had successfully concealed their joy of meeting again by this byplay. As boys they had fought shoulder to shoulder, but fate had separated their trails in later years. Jim Allen was an outlaw, while Jack was a Wyoming sheriff. Now, once more, they were on the same side of the fence, and their joy was unbounded.

"Gosh, there's Toothpick. How are you, you long-legged galoot? An' Sam Hogg—an' Kansas Jones." Allen grinned at his old friends. "What you fellers doin' down here?"

"We read how you was a Ranger captain, so we come along to keep you from gettin' hurt," "Toothpick" chortled.

"We aim to keep you from gettin' swell-headed," Jack cut in.

"I'm darn glad to see you all, and sure need your guns, but—" He stopped and looked at Sam Hogg.

Sam Hogg was a little wiry man with a leathery face, close-cropped white hair, and small, bright eyes. He was an old-time Ranger, but he was now past sixty. So Allen looked at him dubiously.

"You may be a Ranger captain, but that don't make

you boss of all creation," Sam Hogg flared indignantly. "You're figurin' I'm too old, but the governor don't. I'm a regular appointed Ranger, so don't show no lip."

Allen shrugged and grinned. Two of the drivers of the wagons elected to accompany Allen on his raid. But the third, a man called "Blackie," sullenly decided to stay behind. Allen delegated Blackie and one Ranger to remain on the knoll to watch the horses.

That was where Jim Allen made his first slip. It was a mistake which was to prove a costly and almost fatal one.

The teams were harnessed to the three wagons, and they lumbered down the slope, turned into Crawling Creek Trail, and headed for town.

"Kansas" Jones drove the first wagon, while the regular drivers attended to the others. The four Rangers rode as an escort. The Allen brothers and the other men were concealed inside the wagons.

Allen planned to have the wagons go straight down the center street, as if intending to pass through. They were to time themselves so as to be opposite Sheeny Mike's and the hardware store when the attack started. Then, at a signal, they were to leap out and storm the hardware store, thus seizing the reserve ammunition of the town.

If Allen had seen the dust cloud which circled about the slower-moving wagons his suspicions might have been aroused. But as he was within the covered wagon, he failed to see. So they went all unsuspectingly into a deadly trap.

The streets of the town looked normal when the wagons rattled across the bridge over Crawling Creek. Allen glanced out between the flap. He saw nothing out of the ordinary. Loafers lounged about, Mexican women with baskets did their shopping, and a few saddled horses were fighting flies at the hitch rack.

The wagons were close to the hardware store when hell broke loose. A storm of bullets beat against the wagons like hail.

Cyrus C. Thompson and Slim Mason had sprung their trap.

"COME ON, WOLVES!"

CYRUS THOMPSON AND SLIM MASON HAD BEEN EATING breakfast in the Chinese restaurant opposite Sheeny Mike's place when Blackie rode furiously into town. He jerked his horse to a sliding stop, hit the ground with a jump, and banged through the swinging doors of a saloon.

"Where's Slim and Thompson?" he bellowed at the bartender.

"Over at the chink's," the startled man grunted. "What's up?"

Blackie burst into the restaurant and stumbled up to Slim and Thompson.

"The Wolf and the Rangers are coming," he blurted.

"When? Where?" the two snapped.

"They're hidin' in the wagons comin' across the bridge now."

"How many?"

"The Wolf, three regular Rangers, and six gunmen. I got a job like you tole me, drivin' a wagon. This mornin' Allen an' two others come to camp. They had a war talk about surprisin' you fellers. I heard some of what they said, but not all. The other two drivers, the darned fools, threw in with the Wolf. But me—I stayed

33

behind with a kid Ranger to ride herd on their hosses. I let 'em get away"—he hesitated, then continued with a hyenalike grimace—"then I beefed the Ranger and lit out for town."

"They're three regulars, seven gunmen and two drivers. That's all?" Slim demanded sharply.

"That's all I seen."

"Then we got 'em," Thompson barked, and smashed his pudgy hand on the table.

"We'll clean 'em up complete," Slim said savagely.

"Slim, go out and collect the boys. Put 'em on the roofs and in the windows of the stores around Sheeny's place. Blackie, go over and get Dutch. Tell him to take the boys in the saloon up to the roof and tower. They're to stay hid until I give the signal. We'll let the wagons get close, then we'll give 'em hell."

"Good-by, Wolf," Slim cried.

"Tell the boys to act natural. Tip the townfolks off that something is goin' to break, but don't tell 'em what or when. Just tell 'em to keep their guns handy."

Thompson leisurely emptied his coffee cup, then sauntered out after them. He glanced down the street and saw the three wagons just starting across the bridge.

His smile was cruel and crafty. They were moving very slowly. He had plenty of time to place his men before they arrived. He crossed to the hardware store and entered. He found Laughing Ed Cummins and two other men there. He told them crisply what was to happen.

They gave a gleeful shout, leaped the counter, and helped themselves to shotguns. They silenced the proprietor's protest with curses. They ripped open boxes of cartridges and stuffed them into their pockets.

"There ain't nothin' like buckshot and a scatter gun

for street fightin',," Laughing Ed cried, and made the room rock with his laughter.

"Laughin' Ed, downin' these Rangers is sure goin' to make a howl," Thompson said seriously.

"Better have a howl than a Wolf," Laughing cried.

"But the papers—" Thompson began.

"To hell with the papers! They'll have to print the story we tell 'em," Laughing replied.

"Mean' there won't be no live Rangers to contradict us!" Thompson cried, and his eyes sparkled.

"Sure." Laughing faced the other two men. "Don't you hombres forget. Today the only good Ranger is a dead Ranger."

"You're wipin' 'em out?" one man exclaimed.

"Yep, an' keep on shootin' until you're darn sure none of 'em is playin' 'possum."

Laughing Ed Cummins lifted a heavy case in front of the door, then kneeled behind it. The two men took up a position at the window. Cyrus Thompson selected a rifle, then stuffed the magazine full of shells and headed for the stairs.

"Hold your fire, gents, until I give the signal," he warned.

He climbed the stairs and entered a bedroom at the front. He raised the window and peered cautiously into the street. Slim Mason waved to him from the opposite window. By that he knew everything was set. Armed men were at every window and on the roofs.

The wagons were very close now. There was little wind, and the dust covered them in a blanketing cloud. A Ranger rode beside each wagon.

Thompson again peered from the window and glanced up and down the street. He frowned when he saw two dust clouds swirling across the plain straight for the town. One was coming from the north, and the other from the south. He could not see what caused them.

"Some of the boys comin' to town maybe," he said nervously.

Then he dismissed everything but the oncoming wagons from his mind. The first one was opposite him now. He kneeled down and steadied his rifle on the window sill. The first one passed, and he caught the driver of the second on his sights.

He waited for another second, then gently squeezed the trigger.

The report of the rifle sounded like a cannon in the room. He felt the recoil against his shoulder and saw the driver pitch sidewise and fall limply across the wheel.

His single rifle shot was followed by a hurricane of lead. Fire and smoke leaped from windows and roofs. All three Rangers went down before that first volley.

Kansas Jones was the only driver to escape. Long years of being hunted had developed his sixth sense very keenly. This sense cried a warning as he passed the hardware store. Then, just as Thompson fired the opening shot, Kansas saw a flash of a rifle barrel. He threw himself sidewise and landed on all fours in the dust of the road.

The street was a bedlam of kicking, squealing horses and screaming, wounded men. There was the deafening racket of rifle fire.

Thompson shouted at the picture of wild confusion. Then, just as he threw another shell into his rifle, two small men catapulted from the wagon, and their guns were in action before their feet hit the ground. Thompson saw one of them flip up a gun.

A stream of fire flared from it, something smashed against his jaw, and he fell backward into an endless stretch of blackness.

Silent Sam Henry had been riding with Jim and Jack Allen in the wagon driven by Kansas Jones. Thus he was to learn what made the Allen twins such peerless fighting men. Their reactions were those of wild animals.

The echo of the first shot had hardly smashed across the street when they were on their feet, diving out of the wagon. They both caught themselves in mid-air and landed on their feet like two cats. Their guns had started to blaze even while they were in the air.

Silent Sam tumbled out after them. He saw them standing back to back, firing first one gun then the other at blurred shapes in the windows and roofs.

All the wagon horses were down, as well as those of the Ranger escort. Silent saw one Ranger try to crawl to the protection of the wall, then collapse and lie still. Lieutenant O'Brien was pinned down by his dead horse. Supporting himself on one elbow, he was firing at the opposite roof. Dead drivers lay sprawled in the dust. Kansas Jones was crouching beneath the first wagon firing from the scanty protection of a wheel. Up ahead, three figures charged through the smoke and dust, toward them.

"Give 'em hell!" he heard old Sam Hogg whoop exultingly. "Show 'em what the Rangers was once—all teeth and fangs!"

DEATH TOLL

SILVER CONKLIN, HATLESS, WHITE HAIR BLOWING IN the breeze, legs spread apart, coolly worked a Winchester, which he fired from his hip. Kansas Jones jerked backward, then tried desperately to raise his gun, firing finally into the ground. He dashed his hand across his eyes and gathered his fast-failing strength. Though fatally wounded, he fought gamely to keep up.

A black-bearded man, shotgun in hand, rushed from the Chinese restaurant and discharged both barrels into his head. Shouting hoarsely, Silent threw a swift shot at the black-bearded man and missed. As in a dream, he heard Jim Allen's voice.

"Take her easy, kid," the Wolf encouraged.

The black-bearded man was leaping back to the shelter of the restaurant. Allen flipped up his gun. It spat flame and lead. The man staggered over to a railing, clawed at it, and sank slowly to the sidewalk.

Silent Sam glanced swiftly about. He saw Sam Hogg stagger, drop his gun, then pitch head-first into the dust. Jim Allen's face was smeared with blood. His left arm dangled at his side, and blood trickled down his fingers. But with his other gun, he was firing steadily at the flashes coming from the hardware shop. Jack Allen was coolly reloading his empty gun.

Furious rage seized Silent when he saw Silver Conklin. The old outlaw had never opened his mouth since the fight started. His mouth was now hanging loosely open, and Silent knew he had been hit, and hit hard. His face was convulsed like that of an exhausted runner. Yet he methodically fired and reloaded his rifle.

38

Sheer grit was all that kept him on his feet. His rifle boomed, and a man sagged across a window sill in an upper room.

Jack Allen finished reloading his guns. He glanced up, then spun about and went down in a heap.

Silent heard Jim Allen cry out. There was nothing human about that cry—it was savage, animal-like!

Allen's eyes were like those of a wolf now, deep wells of yellow fire. There was something horribly mechanical, yet deadly, in everything he did.

Toothpick staggered, tripped on Jack Allen's prone body and sprawled in the road. Silent saw Jim Allen shove the lanky rider's legs roughly aside, gather up his brother's loaded guns, and once more start to fire.

Only three men remained on their legs. All the others were down. Silver Conklin was as good as dead, but refused to succumb. He was so weak that the recoil of his rifle made him stagger each time he fired. But he continued to fire with deadly effect. Then he lurched sidewise, and Silent knew he had been hit again. His rifle fell unheeded and sent up a little cloud of dust.

Seating himself on the edge of the sidewalk, he fumbled for the "makings." His fingers were all thumbs, but he managed to pull a cigarette paper from his pocket. Then his fingers relaxed. The paper fluttered to the ground. He slumped backward and was dead before his head touched the pavement.

Silent could hear nothing. He could see the flashes of the guns, but he could not hear the reports. Bullets spattered into the dust at his feet. A bullet creased his side. And always there was the picture before him of Allen, firing and firing.

A continuous stream of fire and smoke seemed to

39

leap from Allen's gun. That gun empty, he would grab up another from some limp hand. He flipped up the gun and fired. From behind the low false front of a building a man leaped. He threw up his arms, then dived into the street below.

A group of shouting men appeared through the cloud of smoke. Allen's gun swung on them and they were gone. Then Silent Sam saw Laughing Ed Cummins framed in the doorway of the hardware store. Silent forgot everything else and concentrated on his enemy.

Every one was down except Allen and himself. They were beaten. He was going to die, but he would take Laughing with him. His lips drew back, and he gave a doglike snarl.

The two fired almost instantaneously. Both missed. Silent fired again and saw Laughing stagger. Then a smashing blow caught him on the shoulder. He tried to raise his gun and couldn't. He dashed his hands across his eyes and searched vainly for his enemy. But the doorway was empty. He felt himself sinking through endless space. Jim Allen was on his knees, groping in the dust for another gun.

Silent felt he was dying, but that did not matter. They had been licked. He was too exhausted to care about anything but that. Then a cry cut through the fog of his consciousness and brought him back to life with a jerk.

"Come on, wolves!" the cry came.

He glanced up and down the street, then raised his two clenched hands and echoed that cry:

"Come on, wolves!"

Coming from the north and south, two long strings of riders were converging on the wagons.

The outlaw legion had arrived!

Each member of the legion rode with loose reins or held them in his teeth as he fired right and left. They came without any appearance of hurry, at a slow, steady gallop, and their fire was as regular and deadly as that of a machine gun.

Wild with hysterical excitement, Silent seized Jim Allen by the arm and pointed.

"Come on, wolves!" he croaked. "Show your teeth."

When that cry first went up, little knots of men had been swarming from the adjoining houses. Convinced that the fight was over, they were eager as hounds to be in at the kill. The Wolf was down, blinded by blood, groping fruitlessly in the dust for a loaded gun. A dozen guns were trained on him, but each man withheld his fire until closer. Each was eager for the honor of finishing the Wolf. Then that cry came and was echoed up the street:

"Come on, wolves!"

With that cry, their victory was turned into defeat.

They started and were held motionless by sheer surprise. A few fired at the galloping riders, but the majority went into a panic-stricken flight. They jammed in the doorways, screamed and fought like wild men to escape from the street. The riders poured a pitiless stream of lead into their backs.

One man, braver than his comrades, or perhaps driven crazy by fear, fired point-blank at Bad Bill Rogers and hit his horse in the head. As his mount sank down, Bad Bill flipped up one of his guns and shot the man through the chest. The man collapsed to his knees. Bad Bill stepped away from his fallen horse and coolly shot the fellow through the back of the head.

Silent saw the Yuma Kid thrust his gun close to the face of a wounded man and pull the trigger. The man's face became a red smear as he pitched to the ground.

"They are wolves!" Silent sobbed.

Allen was on his feet again, directing the clean-up. The Yuma Kid, followed by three or four others, charged into Sheeny Mike's saloon. A flurry of shots and the place was taken. Other members of the outlaw legion, pairing off in couples, burst into adjoining houses and stores.

As they entered the front doors, the outlaws scurried out at the back like so many frightened rats. One man, trapped in an upstairs room, became panic-stricken and hurled himself through a closed window. He landed on the sidewalk in a shower of glass and howled with the pain of a broken shoulder.

Someone ended his cries as casually as if he were a wounded buck. The two Cole brothers, rifles in hand, stood on the steps of the saloon, and fired up and down the street at everything which moved.

Five minutes after the outlaw legion galloped into town, the last shot was fired. The townfolk cowered in their houses. Some of the outlaws managed to secure horses and galloped from town as if pursued by the devil. Others were dragged from cellars, barns, and other holes and locked up in the old storeroom behind Sheeny Mike's bar.

"You got five minutes. Then I'm stretchin' your necks," Allen told them savagely.

"Stringin' 'em all up?" Corporal Tait demanded in horror.

"Yeah, they got Jack!" Allen replied flatly.

"They got Jack?" the Yuma Kid said regretfully.

"I knew the way he dropped he was done for."

"I always told you you were too damn smart—you think

42

you know everythin'! You darn little dressed-up dude!"

Jim Allen turned and gaped at his brother. Jack Allen's face was ghastly white. Excepting for a few superficial wounds, he was untouched.

"What you doin' here?" he gasped.

"Where you want me to go? Out in the street to lay down dead—just so you can go on boastin' you know everythin'?" Jack cried weakly.

Jim gulped. "Huh, so you played yellow? Lay down and pretended dead?"

Jack pointed to the buckles of his crossed belts which lay directly over the pit of his stomach. They were torn and bent where bullets had hit them.

"Pretended? Hell, a thousand mules kicked me so darned hard that I went up so high it took me all this time to get down again," Jack said querulously. "What did you do with my guns, you darn thief?"

"Huh," Jim grinned back. "I dunno! They was empty, and some gent took a likin' to 'em. So I threw 'em at him. One went right down his throat."

Then they counted the costs.

Lieutenant O'Brien and his two Rangers were dead. Kansas Jones and the two drivers were also dead. Toothpick and Sam Hogg were dangerously, though not fatally, wounded. Silent Sam had a hole in his leg and a broken shoulder. Besides a bruised stomach, Jack Allen had two other superficial wounds, while Jim had been hit five times though none of his wounds were serious enough to cause much worry.

"Folks sure laugh a lot about my bein' peanut size." Jim stopped and grinned up at the towering Bad Bill Rogers. "If you had been in my place each one of them wounds would have been plum' serious."

43

"Come here, Jim. Old Silver is shot to pieces," one of the Cole brothers called out.

Jim Allen looked down at the dead man. "I know. The first one what hit him was fatal. He was dead on his feet after that, but his nerve kept him up, an' he sure used that rifle of his," Allen said softly.

The rescuing party had two casualties. One Ranger and "Dude" Malone had been killed.

Doc Candee spoke briskly:

"If one of you boys will help, I'll go fix me a surgery and get set to patch you all up."

Tom Cole responded quickly. In a few minutes Toothpick and Sam Hogg were carried into the saloon and placed on a large table.

Pat Garrett glanced around at the sprawled bodies of the dead outlaws.

"We lost quite a few, but from the looks of things, they don't owe us nothin'," he said reflectively.

"Huh, she sure must have been real hot."

"Middlin' so. The Rangers and the drivers was knocked off afore we knew the thing had started," Silent exclaimed.

"Meanin' there was only six of you to go on with the fight," Bad Bill said as he again glanced about the littered street. "Son, you've been in a fight to tell your kids about."

"Yeah, you sure can brag when you get old. Gents what never was near here will be tellin' about this fight," Pat Garrett said slowly. "But, Jim, why did you start afore we arrived?"

"Shucks, they was on to us. I had just tole Kansas to pull up and pretend to water the hosses when they cut loose," Allen said softly as his eyes roamed about the circle.

"Meanin' there's a yellow-bellied traitor among us?"

Allen shrugged. "A couple of you boys go bring in the hosses. Then some of you herd them coyotes out here and start cleanin' up this mess."

Someone called to Allen from the saloon. He went in and found that the doctor had finished dressing the others' wounds and was waiting for him.

Allen stripped off his shirt, and the Rangers who were present gasped. Even Doc Candee, who had seen many gunshot wounds in his turbulent life, whistled softly when he saw Allen's torso. It was covered both back and front by long white welts left by knife wounds and the puckered scars of bullet wounds.

"Yeah, a few gents can shoot straight," Allen said with a grin.

THE AFTERMATH

WHEN THE YUMA KID AND PETE BORDEN RETURNED with the horses, they knew who had been the traitor. They had the body of the young Ranger who had been left in charge of the horses strapped across a saddle. He had been shot through the back of the head at close quarters.

"So that's how they knew!" Allen muttered as Doc finished dressing his wounds.

He walked out of the saloon, and his eyes flared yellow when he saw Blackie among the prisoners who were busily cleaning up the mess in the street. He warned the guards to keep a sharp eye on Blackie, then reentered the saloon.

Before nightfall all signs of that epic struggle had been removed. Nothing remained except the bullet

45

marks in the walls, red stains on the sidewalk, and the long row of fresh graves in Boot Hill. All those who had fallen—outlaws and Rangers—were buried there, except Silver Conklin. He was to be buried in Sunset City.

"Jim," Pat Garrett said with a touch of regret in his voice, "I figure the job is finished. You hit those fellers so hard they'll never get set again. So we'll all be splittin' up again soon."

"Pat"—and Allen did not realize how prophetic his words were—"we didn't get one of their leaders. This job ain't finished until we land Laughin' Ed Cummins, Slim Mason, Cyrus Thompson and the big boss way up top of this devil's gang. An' that time is a long way off."

"Meanin' us wolves has to lick our wounds and wait patient until we has another chance to show our fangs," Doc Candee said.

"What are you goin' to do with the prisoners?" George Cole asked.

"Have 'em tried regular."

"Those fellers own the court. They'll just be turned loose," Pete Borden growled.

"Sure, we'll start playin' the game lawful. Then, if that don't work, we'll try the law of the wild—the law of the tooth and fang!"

On the following morning, in the far-off State capital, both papers, the *Star* and the *Clarion*, spread the story of that fight all over their front pages. The *Clarion* referred to the Rangers as murderers who had ridden into a peaceful, law-abiding town and shot down unarmed citizens. Editorially it declared that nothing else could be expected of a gang of cutthroats led by the Wolf and masquerading as Rangers.

46

However, the *Star* gave the real story, and it was the one the majority believed. It had a ring of sincerity about it. Some man who knew how to write told the story of Silver Conklin's death—told in simple language the old outlaw's desire to redeem his name for the sake of his daughter, and of his other wish, that having once been a Ranger, he might die one. The story read:

Wounded unto death, he fought on, fought against overwhelming odds, and, in dying, gained the victory. He died a man and a Ranger. Let us forget all else.

The governor read it and stared out of the window, visualizing the fight. Then he looked at his brother and smiled grimly.

"Did you notice there were no wounded taken on either side?" he asked.

"Yeah, maybe those fellers just shot straight. Then maybe they didn't want to be bothered with prisoners until the show was over."

"The *Clarion* is raising a terrible storm," the governor said anxiously. "Maybe I'd better wire Allen to ride easy for a while."

"I'm goin' down there," Captain Harrison said decisively as he leaped to his feet.

"To warn Allen to go slow?"

"Hell, no! I missed that scrap, but maybe there'll be another as good. If there is, I'm goin' to be in it," the captain growled.

About the same time that Captain Harrison took a train for Cactus County, Jim Allen, with several of his riders, was watching the arrival of two stagecoaches

47

crowded with men and escorted by a score of riders. Silent Sam suddenly rapped out an oath and pointed.

"There's that big bum, Laughin' Ed Cummins." He cursed freely. "I was hopin' I'd dropped him."

"An' he's wearin' a deputy sheriff's star. What do you figure it means, Jim?" George Cole asked.

"Seein' we licked 'em with bullets, they aim to use the law to lick us," Allen replied.

The men lapsed into silence as they watched the cavalcade file past.

"Slim Mason and Thompson is with them," Silent growled.

The stagecoaches and riders pulled up before a half-ruined church at the farther end of the town. Then the men started to carry books and boxes from the stagecoaches into the building.

"Now what are they up to?" Silent grunted.

They had not long to wait. Before half an hour had passed, they saw Laughing Ed Cummins swinging down the street straight for the Rangers' headquarters. His right arm was in a sling, but he wore a gun tied down to his left side.

"Mornin', gents," he boomed.

He faced the group on the steps quite fearlessly. Allen looked at him. He was bristling with vitality, and Allen realized that the man, having found foes worthy of his steel, was enjoying himself.

"You boys sure put up a good scrap," he cried at last in a voice which could be heard all over the town.

Silent nodded at Laughing's bandaged arm and said brutally:

"I see I nicked you."

Laughing Ed threw back his head and his laugh rang down the street.

"You nicked me? How come? Meanin' I was in the fight?" He chuckled, and his chuckle was louder than most men's laughter. "Mister, you must have been smoke-blind I wasn't in town yesterday."

Silent Sam touched his own bandaged shoulder and snarled:

"Huh, you wasn't in town?"

"Nope—got a dozen witnesses to prove it," Laughing boomed and laughed again.

The faces of the members of the outlaw legion tightened, but Allen only grinned. He admired the man's cool effrontery.

"That so? Then how did you get that arm? Silent sneered.

Laughing Ed switched his eyes and looked directly at Silent. His eyes were still shining, but like ice in the sun.

"That arm? Let's say a skunk bit me. I pay my debts, and I aim to kill that skunk some day," he cried.

"Some day? Why not today?" Silent challenged.

He took a step forward, but Allen pushed him back. Laughing was arrogant and brazen, and Allen did not blame Silent for the challenge, but he could not allow him to fight now in the presence of the whole village.

Laughing was an officer of the law and stood alone in the midst of five Rangers. If Silent killed him, the whole village would swear that it was murder. Then, too, Allen was not at all certain that Silent would win in a gun fight with Laughing. He stepped directly in front of the wrathful Silent and looked at Laughing.

"What you want?" he demanded.

"You've got some prisoners. I've come for them," Laughing said coolly, and completely ignored the ejaculations his demand called forth. "I'm a county

49

officer. Judge Hancock is ready to open court. I've got a court order here for you to turn the prisoners over to me, so they can be committed before the court. If you'll make out the charges, the judge will listen to 'em."

"An' turn 'em loose pronto," Bad Bill laughed.

"Not unless they ain't guilty," Laughing retorted mockingly.

"What'll you do if we don't turn 'em over?" Silent taunted.

"I brought a few deputies with me, an' they ain't coyotes like those gents you wolfed yesterday. I reckon I would have to follow the court order and take 'em by force," Laughing cried. Every word was a deliberate taunt.

This was like a red flag to a bull. The men's faces tightened and their eyes glinted dangerously. Allen thought quickly. Laughing had been sent there purposely to taunt them in the hope that they would refuse to obey the court order. If they did, he would gladly use force, and he would have public opinion on his side.

Allen walked to the door and called:

"Corporal, bring out them gents. Then take them to the court and make out the charges."

Allen caught a look of disappointment on Laughing's face. He looked as if he were about to say something further, then thought better of it and clamped his lips shut. But his laugh boomed out again as the corporal herded his prisoners down the street, and his laugh was sneering, contemptuous. Allen felt his men stir restlessly behind him.

"Damn laughin' hyena!" Bad Bill snarled. "I'd love to swap lead with him."

"Me, too," Pat Garrett gritted.

"He was tryin' to rile you fellers. Don't let him get your goats," Allen grinned cheerfully.

Corporal Tait was back within the hour.

"That damn judge is so crooked he would fit inside a corkscrew. I charged 'em with muder and resistin' an officer, an' the judge turned 'em all loose on fifty-dollar bail," he spluttered wrathfully.

"Which means we don't take any more prisoners," Bad Bill said grimly.

"What's the game now, Jim? You ain't goin' to let Blackie get away with killin' that kid Ranger?" Pat Garret demanded.

"Nope. I want you fellers to think. Is Blackie, Slim Mason or that tub of fat, Thompson, wanted anywhere out of this State?" Allen asked.

"Blackie and Slim Mason is wanted in Mexico," the Yuma Kid replied promptly.

"Say, Kid, wasn't Thompson mixed up in the murder of Mendoza, the rancher, down in Sonora five or six years ago?" Pete Borden asked.

"He sure was. The Mex government is sure anxious to get hold of all three," Yuma replied.

"You sure?" Allen's eyes were shining.

"Just as sure as I'm standin' here."

"Then we got 'em," Allen cried delightedly.

"How come?" the men chorused, loud and vigorously.

"Gents, I didn't care a darn about turnin' loose those coyotes. Silver Conklin was a friend of mine, and I want the gents what downed him. Slim Mason an' Thompson was responsible, even if they didn't pull the trigger. So I'm gettin' 'em."

"Goin' to wolf 'em? Jim don't forget the governor's backin' you, an' you won't do him any good by killin'

51

his political enemies. Even his backers will raise hell if you do that," Bad Bill warned.

"Sorta looks as if they've got us licked, Jim. If we arrest 'em, the judge will turn 'em loose pronto, an' if we drop 'em, we put the governor in bad," Pat Garrett lamented.

"Supposin' I drop 'em lawful, before witnesses, for resistin' arrest?" Allen's eyes were quizzical.

"Why should they resist? They ain't got nothin' to worry about, with that judge sittin' at their trial?" Silent objected.

"That's where Blackie comes in," Allen retorted. "I want you boys to nab him secret."

Then Allen explained his plan, and the men's faces became animal-like as they listened.

THE BLOOD TRAIL

IT WAS SHORTLY AFTER DUSK THAT THE YUMA KID thrust Blackie into the saloon and announced laconically:

"Here he is, Jim."

"What you mean by arrestin' me? I was turned loose by the judge. I'll sue you for illegal arrest," Blackie growled threateningly.

"We're arrestin' you for somethin' else," Allen said coldly.

"All right, take me afore the judge, then. You don't dare do nothin' to me," Blackie blustered.

He would have cowed and whined for mercy before the Wolf in any other circumstances, but he had no fear of the Wolf in a Ranger's uniform. That tied Allen's hands. He was bound to do everything regularly, lawfully.

"Blackie, I'm arrestin' you for murder. You shot that kid Ranger through the back of his head like a dog. You're payin' for that," Allen said tonelessly.

There was something about Allen's voice that made Blackie shiver. A horrible premonition seized him, but he still tried to bluster.

"You ain't got no proof. If you have, tell the judge about it."

"Nope, Blackie, the judge ain't goin' to hear this. You're goin' to act plum' foolish, Blackie. You're goin' to try and escape from me. You're goin' to ride across the border to escape. But that's goin' to be right foolish of you, 'cause Lieutenant Casey of the rurales is goin' to be waitin' for you."

"Casey? You're turnin' me over to him? You ain't got no right—it's against the law," Blackie cried out in a panic.

"You're goin' to be foolish and cross yourself; or, at least, that's what the witness will figure."

Blackie's mouth dropped open and he stared. His eyes became wells of fear. He had heard of Casey of the rurales. He would die within ten minutes after Casey got his hands on him. He dropped to his knees and started to blubber.

"No, no, it's plain murder to turn me over to that tiger. You ain't got no right. I'll confess—tell everythin' about Thompson. He paid me to spy on the Rangers."

"Blackie, you got to pay for that dead kid. Besides, I need you to make them coyotes resist arrest," Allen finished.

The sun, a great golden ball, hung low over the Bear Mountains as all that was mortal of Silver Conklin left the Casa Modoc for the last time. Outlaw, killer, Ranger, he was on his last ride.

The air was warm and fragrant, and the courtyard was full of flowers. Other flowers were heaped in profusion on the rough coffin in the buckboard.

Stella Conklin and the minister's wife walked directly behind the improvised hearse. Behind them came Captain Harry Harrison and four of the outlaw legion in spic-and-span uniforms. Then the whole village—men, women and children, as well as a group of long riders—trailed along behind.

By the way in which he met his death, Silver Conklin had won the forgiveness and respect of all his neighbors. They forgot his past history and only remembered how he had died. They were honest folk who had suffered from the heavy hand of the outlaws who had a strangling grip on the county. Silver had given his life trying to loosen that hand, and now they were honoring him.

Women had stripped their gardens to make wreaths; men had stopped their work to pay him homage. And the girl whom they had formerly scorned they now pitied from the depths of their hearts.

The cortège wound its way down the sunlit street to the little white church. The service was half over when Jim Allen and the Yuma Kid entered. The people forgot the minister and turned and stared at them.

Both looked drawn and tired, and were covered with dust from their long ride. Their faces were sober and very serious. The minister droned on to the end of the simple service. Then the Rangers carried the casket out of the church and lowered it into a grave beneath a giant mulberry tree. Allen walked over to the grave and then turned and faced the crowd.

"Ladies an' gents, you all know how Silver died. He was a fighter and a man. Just keep rememberin' that."

He paused, and then looked down at the bare wooden box. "Silver, you done your part, an' I promise to finish it for you."

Stella Conklin was quietly crying, but pride tempered her grief. Allen saw Silent place his hand on her arm, then, as the girl leaned against him trustingly, around her waist. Silent's face was grave and sorrowful. He had lost a friend. But the bitter lines about his mouth were gone, and his eyes held a new light. Silver Conklin had reached the end of his trail, but a new and brighter one lay at Silent's feet.

SILVER CONKLIN
LIVED LIKE A MAN AND DIED LIKE A RANGER

A cross bearing that inscription was placed at the head of the grave. It bore no date, nothing but those few words. But that was sufficient.

The group broke up and straggled out of the courtyard. Bad Bill Rogers caught the Yuma Kid by the arm.

"Did it work?" he asked anxiously.

"It sure did. I took Kid Riker down to the border to see it. Allen don't miss a trick. He waited until a couple of U. S. border-patrol fellers was passin', then turned Blackie loose. Blackie's horse started to run and went slap over the border, where the rurales grabbed him. We saw 'em shoot him a few minutes later. Those border fellers is willin' to swear Blackie went over of his own accord, an' even Kid Riker called him a damn fool for tryin' to escape. Riker's passed on the news to Thompson by this time. He hot-footed it for Carson as soon as I turned him loose."

"Don't tell me how you made Blackie's horse bolt.

It's better for me not to know anything officially," Captain Harrison said crispy. "But I reckon I can guess how it was done."

"So the thing is all set for Slim Mason and Thompson?"

"Yeah, they're givin' a big political shindy in Carson tonight, and the Wolf is arrestin' 'em at the height of the festivities," Yuma explained.

"Meanin' he's downin' 'em for resistin' arrest," Bad Bill said grimly.

"Sure. After what happened to Blackie, they'll resist, all right. They won't take a chance of his pullin' that game on them."

"Slim Mason is fast, an' Thompson ain't no slouch with a gun," Pete Borden said with a frown.

"Yeah, but he's got to play it single-handed, or they won't go for their guns," Yuma said. Then he pointed to a bare slope to the south of the town.

They watched Allen and his grays toil up the slope and vanish over the rim. Then Captain Harrison bestirred himself.

"I'm ridin' to Carson to pick up three or four witnesses to watch this play," he announced.

Cyrus C. Thompson was not at all perturbed when Kid Riker told him about Blackie's end. If the fool had made a bum play and had been caught by the rurales, that was no one's business but his own. He could easily be replaced. He even refused to be worried when Slim Mason told him later in the afternoon that Allen had sworn out warrants charging them both with murder.

"Let him serve them. I want to talk to him, an' will do so when he arrests me," Thompson laughed.

"Goin' to make him an offer?" Slim asked.

56

"Sure, why not? Every man has his price," Thompson said cynically, "I'll offer him a good one. It will be cheaper than fighting him."

"Maybe," Slim said doubtfully, "Listen, boss, you got to stop Allen quick. Buy him or beef him pronto. Since that fight, folks is gettin' quite uppish. You got to do somethin', or the whole county will rise against you."

"Let 'em try it. Anythin' special on your mind?" Thompson growled.

"Ted Strong announced today he's goin' to run for county attorney. He's popular, and folks might get brave an' vote for him," Slim announced.

"He is, is he? Huh, he'll do to teach the fools a lesson. I'll learn them I'm boss of this county in spite of all the damn Rangers in the State," Thompson growled.

He rubbed his fat hands together, and his eyes became cruel like those of a shark. "Ted Strong's got a wife and a sister, ain't he? Yes, an' they're both pretty. You slip the word to Dutch Ogal that he can have 'em, They ought to be worth somethin'. But he's got to make them disappear without leavin' a trace."

"That will sure make Strong behave, and his backers will hunt their holes." Slim smiled evilly.

Having casaully condemned two girls to a horrible fate, the men forgot them and went on to discuss more important affairs.

"A GOOD, HONEST FIGHT"

THAT SAME EVENING CYRUS C. THOMPSON WAS replendent in one of the few evening suits in the county. Diamond studs glittered from his boiled shirt, while a huge diamond flashed from one of his pudgy fingers.

His coat was tight-fitting, so that the bulge made by the gun he wore in a shoulder holster was plainly visible. He carried another gun, a smaller one, in a specially made pocket on his hip.

Slim Mason stood close to him. He wore his gun tied low on his thigh.

Thompson and Slim both stood by the door of the big dance hall and greeted the guests as they arrived.

Thompson was hearty and affable. The elite of the town, both men and women, were present. Many of them were his henchmen. Others came because they feared to make themselves conspicuous by their absence.

Ted Strong was a man of thirty-five with a resolute face. His wife and his sister were both exceptionally pretty women in their early twenties. Thompson greeted them with a sharklike grin.

"Hear you're goin' to run on the opposition ticket, Strong?" Thompson spoke genially, and added hypocritically:

"I like a good, honest fight."

"You'll get a fight, all right—it's up to you whether it's an honest one or not," Strong replied bluntly.

Thompson laughed with pretended good humor, but the two women shrank back when they saw the expression that came into his eyes as he looked at them.

"Make yourselves at home, folks. You'll find refreshments in that room back of the palms," Thompson invited.

Strong and the women made way for a crowd of new guests.

"His eyes—they frighten me," his wife shuddered.

"He's a devil. Why did we come here?" his sister cried.

"Captain Harrison asked me to come as special favor. He said the Wolf was going to arrest both of those fellows, and wanted me to see him," Strong replied.

Cyrus C. Thompson turned to Slim Mason and whispered harshly:

"Did you hear him? Honest election! Damn him, defying me to my face. He wouldn't have dared to do that before those damned Rangers came. We got to stamp this out pronto."

Slim Mason's white face resembled that of a corpse, but his eyes were alive with evil joy.

A man hurried into the dance room.

"Boss, the Wolf came to town a while ago," he gasped.

"Is he comin' here?"

"He tole Spike he was, but he's sittin' over in the Mexican restaurant eatin' supper as peaceful as you please, right now."

"Let him come and serve his damn warrant." The judge is waitin' to bail me out," Thompson laughed arrogantly.

It was close to midnight, and the dance was at its height when Allen appeared.

The floor was crowded with gay couples, the band was playing a lively tune, and shouts of merriment came from the refreshment room.

Jim Allen looked very young and boyish as he stood framed in the doorway. He seemed pitifully small and frail in his tight-fitting uniform. The side of his head was covered with plaster, and his left hand and arm were bandaged. He wore but one gun on his right side. His freckled face was grave but untroubled.

59

"The Wolf!" a dancer said in a startled whisper.

"That kid? Impossible!" his partner cried.

"It's him, and he means business. Look at his eyes," the man said shrilly.

"Yellow fire! That's why they call him a wolf."

"The Wolf!"

That whisper leaped across the room. The dancers stopped abruptly and gaped at Allen open-mouthed. The music ceased with a discordant crash. As Allen advanced across the floor, the crowd opened before him until there was a straight lane leading to Thompson and Slim Mason. He advanced down this neither slowly nor rapidly, but very deliberately.

"That's him. Strong and you others keep your eyes peeled so you can swear as to what happens," Captain Harry Harrison called.

"Watch? What for?"

"To see him wolf these fellers."

"Murder 'em?" Strong exclaimed in a startled voice.

"No, execute 'em," the captain snapped.

Cyrus Thompson and Slim Mason saw Allen the moment he stepped through the door, and now they stood side by side and waited for him. His advance through that human lane was unhurried, but as implacable as fate itself.

Thompson had an uneasy feeling as he watched Allen. He licked his lips nervously and glanced at Slim Mason's face.

Slim's face was like that of a marble statue. He was supremely confident that, no matter what was to come, he was equal to any emergency. He would best Allen either with words or with guns. He did not underrate the Wolf, but he was positive that he was a split second faster with his gun.

60

Allen advanced very close, stopped, and held out two papers in his bandaged hand.

"Gents, those are warrants. I'm arrestin' you both." Allen hardly spoke above a whisper, yet the stillness in that room was so great that his words carried to the farthest corners.

"On what charge?" Thompson asked, and tried to summon a sneer.

Allen's flaring yellow eyes disconcerted him, filled him with fear, and made it hard for him to collect his thoughts.

"Murder!"

That single word sounded like a clap of thunder.

"A frame-up. Let's go and see the judge and get it over with. I'm anxious to get back to my guests." Thompson laughed, but his laugh was forced.

"You've got a gun—I can see the bulge. And you, too, Mason. Hand yours over," Allen ordered.

"You don't get my gun, Allen, but I'll go with you to see the judge," Slim Mason replied coldly.

"Your guns," Allen said flatly.

"Let's give 'em to him, Slim, and go and see the judge and get it over with," Thompson growled.

Allen lowered his voice so that it only reached the two men.

"We ain't goin' to see the judge."

"Not see the judge? We have a right to ask for bail," Thompson said.

"You're starin' for Four Point pronto. We'll go by the way of Mexico. The border ain't far from Carson." Allen spoke so softly that his lips barely moved.

"Mexico—the border—like hell!" Slim sneered.

"You own the judge. It ain't justice to have him sit at your trial. You two was back of the killin' of Silver Conklin. You downed him, even if you didn't pull the

61

trigger. You're standin' trial for that—a fair an' square trial—not before your crooked judge, but before a Mexican judge."

"You're crazy. You ain't got no right to turn us over to the Mexicans." Thompson was bewildered.

"You gents hear about Blackie?" Allen asked.

"Yeah. The darn fool hopped over the border and the rurales downed him," Slim sneered. "What's that got to do with us?"

"His hoss ran away. Maybe other hosses will do the same!"

Thompson gasped. "You done that? You turned Blackie over to them?"

Allen nodded.

Then they knew. The story of Blackie's end, as related by Kid Riker, leaped into their minds. That had been a trick. Kid Riker had been fooled, and now Allen intended to play the same game over again—with them.

Once they were disarmed he would whisk them out of town and ostensibly start for Four Point Crossing, traveling by way of the border. Allen might eventually reach Four Point, but they never would.

Thompson was bewildered. The yellow fire in Allen's eyes seared into his brain, made it impossible for him to think clearly. One idea leaped into his mind and stayed there. To surrender to Allen meant death. He knew what the rurales would do once they got their hands on Slim and himself.

The veins in his neck stood out like cords, while the color drained from his cheeks, leaving them flabby and white. Arrest meant death—those warrants held by Allen would prove to be their death warrants.

"Gents"—Allen raised his voice until it rang through the room—"I'm a Ranger with authority to make an arrest. Up with your hands, gents. I'm warnin' you I'll have to kill you if you resist."

Slim Mason welcomed the issue. It had been his boast that he would some day best Allen, and here was his opportunity. The fight was forced on him. He would have to draw or die. His self-confidence was supreme. He was faster than the Wolf, and he knew it.

To resist Allen before these witnesses was a serious offense, for he was a Ranger performing his duty. But anything was better than arrest—the border—the rurales—death!

Slim's eyes narrowed. His shoulders sank down in a crouch.

"Gents, reach for the sky. I'm warnin' you fair. I'm countin' three," Allen cried sharply.

Slim's hand moved inch by inch closer to his gun.

"One—"

There was a blur of movement, and Slim's and Allen's hands each came up with a gun. The reports were so blended that they sounded as one. Another shot crashed out, and Slim pitched sidewise against Thompson, who cursed like a crazy man as he flung the body aside. Slim fell as limply as a wet rag, and his gun slithered along the polished floor.

As Allen fired his second shot, he leaped aside as lightly as a cat, so that for one second he was covered by Slim's falling body. Thompson tried desperately to bring his gun to bear, but before he could turn sufficiently, Allen had fired one-two-three times.

Thompson crashed to the floor. For a moment the tableau was shrouded by swirling, choking smoke. Then some woman screamed. There was a stamp of feet as some of the guests rushed toward the door in panic. But the majority were too paralyzed to move. They stood their ground and stared at Allen's crouching figure and the two immovable bodies.

Then Allen commenced to laugh—strange laughter that bit into the onlookers' consciousnesses and filled them with horror. There was nothing human about it—it was mocking, yet mirthless.

Then he shook his head, and his laughter ceased.

"Gents, you saw they resisted arrest," he said softly. "I reckon that's all."

He sheathed his gun, clapped his bandaged hand against his side, and walked slowly toward the door. A dark spot appeared on his uniform; the white bandage reddened.

The crowd opened in front of him. He looked neither to the right nor left. He knew what he would see in their eyes. He had seen it in other men's eyes before—vague fear, the repugnance with which one regards a loathsome spider or a hangman.

So Allen left the hall as he had arrived—alone.

Slowly the spectators recovered their senses. They stared at the dead men in awe.

"I tole you you would witness an execution," Captain Harrison whispered to Strong. "He's fast and sure."

"What made them resist? The fools went for their guns and forced his hand. He warned them," Strong said curiously.

"Lost their heads. Slim's always boasted he was faster than Allen. Now he knows he ain't." A heavyset man laughed brutally. He was one of Thompson's partisans. "Why didn't they surrender peacefully? They had nothing to worry about."

"Must have been plumb crazy resistin' a Ranger. Why do you figure they did it?"

Captain Harry Harrison smiled grimly, but made no reply.

Later that night, Allen sat by a small fire far out in the Cactus Desert. He had dressed the wound in his side and had then forgotten it. His two grays stood unheeded near him.

The fire died down, and the red coals turned to gray ashes, but Allen continued to sit there as immovable as a statue.

Allen was tired—tired and bitter at the role he was always cast to play. He tried to find comfort in the thought of Silent and Stella. A new trail full of promise had opened up for them. He had started their feet along it. But their trail was not for him. His trail stretched straight along into the distance, and no man could see the end. It was red all the way.

He and his wolves would follow it, for his job was not yet finished.

He shook his head, jumped lightly to his feet, pinched Princess's ear, and grinned.

"Reckon we'd better start cleanin' up Sharon County next. Suppose we hit the breeze for Casa Modoc and make them turtledoves give us a bucketful of pancakes?"

He whistled as he saddled his grays. Then, a few minutes later, he was drifting through the silver night, and as he went, he sang softly to himself. He was content again.

THE DOPE GANG

JIM-TWIN ALLEN AND TOOTHPICK JARRICK HAD RIDDEN from Carson, where the Ranger headquarters were located, to Mesa Verde, where the Outlaw Legion was camped. Then he and Toothpick had started to ride over the barrens, searching for clues on their most exciting case since the trouble with the tricky Cyrus Thompson.

Since the death of Thompson, one of their ringleaders, Captain Painton, headed a gang for running dope across the Mexican border. Allen had said that he would never rest until he took this secret leader of the dope ring, Captain Painton.

The sound of gunfire in the distance put Allen on the alert. He had been swaying loosely in the saddle while Princess, his old gray mare, ambled along as though walking in her sleep. A quick change came over the little Ranger and his horse as the faint noise rattled through the hot air. Princess flattened her ears and tossed her wicked head; Allen straightened and turned to face the ragged hills on the horizon.

"Did you hear that, Toothpick?" he asked quickly of his companion.

"Toothpick" Jarrick, a tall, lanky youth, had been watching Allen with keen amusement, half expecting him to tumble to the ground at any moment.

The sudden change that came over Allen mystified him. His smile faded as Allen spoke. He peered around and listened intently.

"Do I hear what?" he retorted dryly, "I hear a fly buzzin' and our saddles creakin', and a cow mooin' somewhere near by, but that's all."

"Shucks, I heard shootin', and I wasn't asleep, either," Allen replied tartly. "It come from over there near Bald Peak. I reckon there was three guns goin' at once, but it's all over now."

Toothpick stared at Allen incredulously. Few men knew the Wolf better than he, yet he was forever finding his friend's animal-like senses a source of wonder. "Aw, you're funnin' with me," he remarked. "I never heard any shootin'."

Allen wagged his head stubbornly. "Somebody's in trouble over there. We better be dustin' it for Bald Peak," he declared.

"You mean to say you could tell where the sound come from, if there was any, and how many guns was makin' it?" Toothpick protested.

"Why, a sense of hearin' like that ain't human. Maybe you can even see from here who it is that's slingin' the lead."

"No, I can't see nothin' from here," Allen answered quickly. "But I know that Doc Candee went ridin' over in that direction alone today, and I got a hunch he was in on that shootin'."

"Doc? Come on, Jim, we'll find out if it's so," Toothpick declared anxiously.

Quickly as his decision was made, he was slower than Allen, who was already kicking Princess's sides and pounding away. The old gray went running smoothly across the dry flat while Toothpick followed as fast as he could.

Toothpick Jarrick had worked shoulder to shoulder with Allen from the beginning. Doc Candee, a close friend of them both, a killer outlaw who had once been a Texas sheriff, was as loyal to the cause. Allen's hunch that Doc was in trouble was more than enough to send Toothpick racing across the flats.

The miles vanished swiftly beneath Princess's galloping hoofs. Toothpick pressed his horse hard to keep up with the old gray. As they rode, twilight settled down over the buttes. Darkness would come quickly, and Allen was riding at top speed in a race against the night.

"There he is, he's comin' down the trail," Allen shouted suddenly.

Toothpick peered through the thickening darkness, trying to see what Allen had discovered.

Suddenly a cry escaped him as he saw a rider come into view at the base of the hills, swinging from behind a thick growth of saplings. The man's mount was running erratically, shifting on and off the trail.

"It's Doc, all right, and he's hurt," Toothpick cried.

"Yeah, some skunk's tried to down him," Allen shouted back as he raced on.

Princess soon covered the intervening distance. Allen leaped off the saddle, ran forward, and caught the bridle strings of the shying pony.

"You hurt bad, Doc?" he cried quickly.

"A couple of the dope-runnin' gang got me in the wing," Doc gasped. "It ain't nothin'. I tried to follow 'em but this danged old nag wouldn't let me."

"You stay in that saddle a minute, Doc," Allen ordered crisply. "Your arm ain't broke, but you've been losin' blood. You've got to be fixed up pronto."

Allen ripped open the sleeve of Doc Candee's shirt and found that the bullet had passed through the flesh of the upper arm and grazed the bone. Allen quickly made a tourniquet with his kerchief and a stick, stopping the bleeding. Then, using Toothpick's bandanna, he bound the wound. When he finished, Doc Candee breathed a sigh of relief.

"You better not waste any more time on me, Jim," he exclaimed. "Them two skunks are ridin' for the border. If you don't head 'em off they'll get across."

Allen looked into Doc's face and said in a cold, hard tone:

"Toothpick and me are slopin' after them two

hombres pronto. How'd it happen, Doc? Talk fast and tell us which way they're headin' for the border."

"I was ridin' through the hills, lookin' for fresh trails and I came across a new one that circles around Bald Peak," Doc answered quickly. "I was followin' it when I heard voices, so I went on easy and listened. There was two gents restin' by the side of the trail. From what I heard 'em say, they was headin' to some meetin' place to see Captain Painton. Seems that the dope-runnin' gang is bandin' together to start a new fight on us, Jim."

"I been waitin' for 'em to do that," Allen remarked flatly.

"I was hopin' that they would say somethin' that would give away where Captain Painton is hidin' out, but things started happenin' so I didn't find out. One of the two hosses belongin' to the pair of dope runners must've smelled my hoss. He let out a whinny, then there was hell to pay. First thing I knew both of them skunks was rushin' down at me and slingin' lead.

"I tried to hold 'em off, but they was too much for me. I got this hole in my arm early in the fight. The shock of the bullet sort of made my mind go blank for a minute. I fell off my hoss. They must've thought I was dead. When I come to, they was poundin' it along the trail, headin' south. I got back into the saddle and started followin' 'em, but I got so dizzy I didn't know where I was goin'. I never knew my hoss was takin' me back to Carson till just a minute ago."

"How does the trail lead to the border?" Allen demanded.

"I reckon it keeps on the other side of the ridge," Candee answered breathlessly. "You'll have to do some fast ridin' to head 'em off, Jim."

"We can reach 'em through Dog Canyon if they ain't
69

still hurryin'," Allen declared grimly. "Can you make it back to Carson alone, Doc?"

"Sure," Doc Candee answered gamely. "Only I'd like to go with you after those runners."

"Nope, you take it easy and get the doctor to fix you up better soon as you hit town," Allen ordered.

He turned quickly and swung into the saddle. Toothpick took the cue and mounted his own horse. He had scarcely slapped into the leather by the time Allen was riding away at full speed.

Dog Canyon lay miles ahead, and it would be pitch black by the time they reached it.

Toothpick never ceased to marvel that Allen could find his way through that treacherous country with such certainty. Once they left the flats and rode into the foothills the going became decidedly dangerous. There were great cracks in the dry ground, and if a horse should stumble into one of them, it would surely mean the death of horse and rider.

Only a faint startlight lighted their way. The course Allen was taking would have been difficult in broad daylight. It became even harder as he plunged up the steep slope, still dodging the dangers that lay in his path. Suddenly they entered the steep-walled Dog Canyon and the darkness became even more oppressive.

Toothpick could no longer see Allen. He had to trust to his horse to follow. Great boulders made the canyon a veritable maze, but still Allen did not slow down. The ride was a nightmare to Toothpick.

Then they rode out of the far end of the canyon. The open ground and the dim light of the stars seemed like blessings to Toothpick. Allen turned sharply and began to climb the slope. Princess bounded ahead with the agility of a goat, while Toothpick's horse labored. When they reached a ledge, Allen sped across it, then whirled and stopped, peering down.

"Here's the trail," Allen exclaimed. "There's fresh marks of hosses headin' south. They've already been through here."

"You've got eyes like a cat's," Toothpick exclaimed. "I can't see anything but black ground."

"Come on, we've got to catch up with 'em," Allen ordered sharply.

They raced ahead at an even faster speed than before. Toothpick realized that their pursuit of the two dope runners had taken a dangerous turn. For the pair of dope runners would probably hear them coming and wait for them in ambush.

At that moment the air rocked with the report of a gun. A vivid flash of flame darted out of the darkness, and a bullet whined past Allen's head. Instantly, Allen spun out of the saddle, and when he struck the ground he was crouching. His Colts came out of his holsters like lightning.

Toothpick also leaped down, but before he could get his gun ready for action, a fusillade of bullets swarmed toward them.

The shots came from behind two boulders at the base of a wall of sheer rock. The dope runners were well protected, while Allen and Toothpick were out in the open. Toothpick uttered a wild shout and dropped flat. Looking around him quickly, he saw another rock a few yards away. He scrambled up and made a dash for it. Once behind it he hunched down breathlessly and looked around for Allen.

"Jim!" he called anxiously.

There was no answer; he could see nothing. For a

moment a horrible fear gripped Toothpick, a fear that Allen had been hit. It threw him into a panic. He peered vengefully across the ledge, hoping to glimpse the outlaws hiding behind the other rocks, but the darkness was so intense that he was unable to see. He could only wait for a chance to throw a bullet at them.

"If they've got Jim I'll keep after 'em as long as I live," he vowed with ominous solemnity.

Then his heart leaped with sudden joy. A voice near by shouted:

"Hang onto your ears!"

It was the voice of Jim-twin Allen. A jubilant shout escaped from Toothpick as he heard it. He knew that somehow Allen had managed to escape the attack and had worked himself into a position from which he could see the two members of the dope-running gang. Toothpick had scarcely a moment to think, for instantly the air shook with the crashing reports of six-guns.

He called Allen's name again and bounded away from the shelter of his rock. He was game to fight in the open if Allen was.

He heard swift movements in the darkness, then two more shots. The flash of flame from one of the guns revealed Allen's face.

"Close in from the other side, Toothpick," Allen cried.

Toothpick obeyed as best he could. He crouched at the base of the wall of rock, drawing back the hammer of his gun, and waiting. It was very quiet now, except for the sound of slow, even footfalls. It was Allen moving. Then a match flared and the yellow light revealed the boulder behind which one of the outlaws had hidden. Near it a man was lying motionless.

"You got one of 'em, Jim," Toothpick shouted.

"Where's the other?"

"He dodged over behind another rock and got away," Allen answered softly.

Toothpick ran forward and stared down at the dead outlaw. The man was lying face up, his mouth agape. Two bullet holes were visible in his black shirt. Toothpick looked up to see Allen's eyes gleaming like a wolf's.

"We better look out for the other one, Jim," he cautioned.

"Nope, he got to his hoss and lit out," Allen explained. "We're headin' after him right now."

Toothpick was only too eager to follow Allen. All of the dope-running gang were desperate characters and as long as any of them remained alive, the job of the Outlaw Rangers was unfinished. Soon they were in their saddles and racing across the ledge.

Allen followed the trail down the hillside until it came to level ground. Then he prodded Princess to her fastest speed. With Toothpick pounding along behind him, he rushed through the thick darkness as silently as a ghost.

Suddenly Allen pulled to a stop. He did this so abruptly that Toothpick had to swing aside to avoid a collision. The lanky Ranger turned back and demanded breathlessly:

"Why're you stoppin', Jim? The border's close now. If we don't keep goin' we'll never catch that coyote."

"Shucks, I'm willin' to let him go," Allen answered gently.

"Let him go? What for? After he tried to kill Doc?" Toothpick asked, aghast.

"I'm gettin' plumb tired of chasin' small fry," Allen answered. "They ain't important; they're only hired by

Captain Painton. As soon as we get rid of some of the gang, he hires more. We ain't ever goin' to break 'em up till we get Captain Painton hisself."

"Yeah, that's true, but we're workin' toward it," Toothpick protested. "We got Laughin' Ed Cummins out of the way, and he was Captain Painton's right-hand man. The time's comin' when you'll get Painton within reach of your guns, too."

"I won't ever do that if I spend all my time chasin' those that work for him," Allen retorted. "After this I ain't goin' to waste any bullets on his hired men. I'm goin' after Captain Painton personal."

"How you goin' to do that?" Toothpick inquired.

"Shucks, I know all about him," Allen answered. "That false beard he wears ain't foolin' me none. He's been layin' low, too, but I know where he's hidin'. I've been pickin' up one clue after another, and today I got the last one I need. Soon as I'm sure he's going to a certain hide-away I know about, I'm goin' there and wolf him."

"Gosh, I never knew you found out all that, Jim," Toothpick exclaimed.

"Yeah, and it's only a question of hours now till I get him," Allen announced. "Come on, Toothpick. We're headin' back to Carson."

Allen turned Princess as he spoke and began riding away. Toothpick talked excitedly. He was never so happy as when his tongue was wagging, and now he had plenty to talk about. He shot question after question at Allen, and when Allen kept quiet he was only spurred to further inquiry. At last, when they were about a mile away from the place where they had abandoned the chase of the "small fry," Toothpick burst out indignantly:

74

"Sometimes your ears is so sharp you can hear a pin drop on a pillow a mile away, but when I ask you for information you don't hear me at all. You're the most exasperatin' cuss I ever saw!"

Allen grinned loosely. "Shucks, Toothpick, don't pay any attention to what I said back there. I wasn't talkin' to you anyway."

"Wasn't talkin' to me!" Toothpick exclaimed. "There ain't nobody else with us that you could've been talkin' to."

"Sure, I was talkin' to that dope runner we was chasin'. He was hidin' in the bushes just a few yards from us when we stopped."

"What? He was?" Toothpick blurted. "You mean to say that skunk was right close to us and you never told me? Why, he might've picked us both off and left us there for the buzzards."

Allen wagged his head. "Nope, I figured he wouldn't do that. We was two agin' his one. He knew we was catchin' up on him, so he dodged out of sight and waited for us to pass. He thought the darkness would cover him, but I seen his tracks turn toward the bushes. He was there, all right. And what I said was for his benefit."

"Didn't you mean those things about Captain Painton?" Toothpick demanded angrily.

"Nope. I don't know who Captain Painton is. I ain't got any more idea of it now'n I had in the first place. I don't know where he's hidin' out, or anything else about him, except that he's the head of the gang and the man I'm after. I said those things to you, figgerin' that our man would hear 'em, and go report what I said to Captain Painton."

"Then what?" Toothpick snapped. "Captain Painton

75

will think you meant it. The first thing you know you'll be gettin' a bullet in your back."

"Yeah, I'm sort of hopin' Painton will try it," Allen answered calmly.

Toothpick gasped. "Jim, have you gone crazy? Are you actually invitin' that devil to try to kill you?"

"Sure, because when he tries it he'll have to come out of his hole," Allen answered. "When he comes out, I'll have a chance of gettin' him. It may be risky, but it's the only way I know of right now of forcin' his hand."

"Gosh, Jim, that's suicide!" Toothpick blurted.

"Yeah. Maybe for me—maybe for Captain Painton," Allen declared.

"ALLEN MUST DIE!"

THE MEMBER OF THE GANG WHOM ALLEN HAD trailed, crouched behind the clump of bushes and listened intently. "Dixie" Kirk did not move until he was sure that Allen and Toothpick were far away. Then he rose, his thin lips curved into a smile of grim satisfaction, and slapped his six-shooter back into its holster.

"So you think you're goin' to get Captain Painton, do you, Allen?" he remarked. "Well, I reckon this is one time you're countin' your chickens afore they're hatched."

He turned and groped through the darkness toward his pony. He had just had time to hide it behind a clump of saplings before Allen had stopped within earshot. He pulled into the saddle and dashed away.

He turned back the way he had come and at last began climbing the slope of the hills. He knew the trail well and was able to follow it without difficulty.

After a short time he forced his horse up the last steep and came upon the ledge. He rode quickly to the spot where the fight with Allen and Toothpick Jarrick had occurred and struck a match. Its light showed him Mace Dodge, lying dead beside the rock.

"Allen's goin' to pay for that," he vowed grimly.

He turned quickly to his pony and untied his blanket roll. After spreading the blanket over the dead man's form, he weighted it down with rocks. Having done this, he returned to his horse and mounted. In a moment he was following the trail southward, heading for lower ground.

Once he was out of the hills, Dixie Kirk rode swiftly. There was a certain swaggering air about him, even when he rode. Any one wise in the ways of the West would have known at a glance that Dixie Kirk was an outlaw and a killer riding the long trail.

Kirk did not suspect that he had fallen into a trap set by Jim-twin Allen. Allen's words, which Kirk had overheard, had been spoken so convincingly that he accepted them at their face value. Now he was riding by a direct route to carry the news to the man who controlled the dope-running gang—Captain Painton.

Though Kirk took every short cut, the ride was a long, wearing one. At no time was he sure that when he arrived he would find Captain Painton at his destination.

Painton's movements were always mysterious; he appeared at one of his many hideaways and, after giving orders or consulting with his henchmen, disappeared again.

Kirk was riding toward a cabin hidden in the Sangre de Dios Mountains, where he had last seen Painton, in the hope that he would still be there.

77

Long past midnight Kirk reached the base of the trail which he knew led to the secret cabin. The narrow path wound up in a circuitous, confusing manner.

At last Kirk reached the entrance to a little-known chasm high above the timber line. It appeared to be only a narrow crack in a wall of rock, but beyond it widened into a great open space, inclosed by sheer walls of rock. It was impossible to ride a horse through the entrance. When Kirk reached it, he dismounted and walked toward the cleft, raising his hands in the air.

Suddenly a sharp, swift command stopped him "Halt! Where you goin'?"

Behind a flat-sided rock near the cleft a man was standing with a rifle. The weapon was pointed squarely at Kirk's chest.

"I'm goin' to see Captain Painton. I've got important news."

The man with the rifle hesitated. Then he asked "What's your name and password?"

"Dixie Kirk. My password is tequila."

A silence ensued. A second man stepped from behind the boulder and conferred with the first. They whispered together a moment, then the second disappeared into the depths of the chasm.

"Jasper, you better be tellin' the truth, or you'll be food for the buzzards," the sentry declared.

Dixie Kirk smiled grimly. He kept his hands elevated until the second man came hurrying back to the crevice. Again there was whispering between him and the rifleman. Then the sentry remarked:

"All right, you can go ahead."

Kirk dropped his arms and strode through the narrow

entrance of the hidden chasm. He began walking toward a light which was burning a hundred yards away.

As soon as he moved, two men stepped out of the shadows and walked with him. Both of them were armed. All this, Kirk knew, was necessary precaution on the part of Captain Painton.

He was escorted all the way to the door of the little weather-blackened cabin which sat in almost the center of the chasm, surrounded by steep rock walls and covered by the sky.

He pushed open the door and stepped inside the cabin. A strong light struck his eyes and he stopped, blinded for the moment. Then he heard the cold, hard voice of Captain Painton.

"You were ordered across the border, Kirk. What do you mean by disobeying and coming back here?"

"One of the Rangers spotted us as we was goin', boss," Dixie Kirk answered evenly. "We put a bullet into him and went on. Then two more trailed us—Jim-twin Allen and Toothpick Jarrick. They killed Mace Dodge, but I got away. I come back here to tell you what I overheard Allen say."

A moment of silence followed Kirk's answer. Captain Painton, hidden in the shadow behind the lamp, was considering his words. Then Painton spoke again:

"What did Allen say, and how did you happen to hear him?"

"He was chasin' me, but I slipped away and hid. In a minute he come along, but he stopped and began to talk to Toothpick Jarrick. He said he knows who you are and where you hide. He said he's been findin' clues, and today he found the last one he needed to get you. He's aimin' to surprise you and take you prisoner."

Again there was a strained silence. When Captain

Painton spoke again his voice was harsh and rasping.

"Leave me here with Kirk," he ordered the two guards. "Be ready to go with him when he comes out."

The two men turned away without a word. Dixie Kirk was alone with Captain Painton.

The shade of the lamp fell into place, and Kirk could see dimly. Behind the table, a man was standing, a gun gripped in his hand, ready for use. Kirk had seen this man before, but he felt a cold chill as acute as that he had experienced when first setting eyes on this remorseless gang leader, Captain Painton.

He saw a man with a thin-tipped mouth, a hawk-like nose, and a face covered with a heavy beard. Kirk knew that the beard was false; in fact, Captain Painton was known to have frankly admitted that it was. But it served its purpose and allowed him to move about in the open without fear of being recognized.

It was Captain Painton's eyes that held Dixie Kirk. They were a pale, chilly gray and glistened with passionless cruelty. But at the same time they denoted self-control and an iron will. Here was a man who would never be stampeded.

"If I learn you're not telling the truth, you'll be eating daisy roots mighty soon, Kirk."

"I'm tellin' you the truth, and you know it," Dixie Kirk answered calmly. "I couldn't fool you with any cooked-up lie. Allen said just what I told you. You've got plenty of reason for wantin' him out of the way. I hate him as much as you do. I'm aimin' to kill him."

"Why?" Captain Painton asked sharply.

"Because he killed Mace Dodge. Mace and me rode the trail together for years. I'm aimin' to make Allen pay for cashin' him."

"Good," Captain Painton said bluntly. "You're right.

80

We both have reasons for wanting to present Allen with a harp." He paused, then asked suddenly:

"Did he mention my name—my real name—and where my hide-out is?"

"No," Dixie Kirk answered. "He never mentioned either one. Even if he did, it wouldn't make no difference to me. All I'm interested in is gettin' Allen. I'm here to make a bargain with you. It's worth a lot to you to have Allen killed, and you'll pay me well to do it."

"Don't try to dictate to me, Kirk!" Captain Painton exclaimed hotly. "I'll handle this matter in my own way. When I decide that you're the man to intrust with the killing of Allen, I'll give you the job, but not before."

"Allen's been fightin' you plenty hard," Kirk answered evenly. "He's took every trick so far. If he ain't cashed pronto, you're finished."

"Allen signed his own death warrant when he came here to fight me. He hasn't stopped me yet and he never will. After he's dead I'll build up my gang as strong as it ever was."

"Not if Allen gets you first, you won't," Kirk said calmly.

"Allen will never touch me," Painton exclaimed. "He's going to die—he must die. I won't permit him to stand in my way a minute longer than necessary. I'll prove to every one that not even Allen can break me."

For the first time Dixie Kirk felt a flash of apprehension. He inwardly recoiled before something he saw in Captain Painton's eyes. It was the hatred of a maniac.

"He's the devil hisself," Kirk thought uneasily.

"Jim Allen must go, or he'll break down my work of years," Captain Painton said crisply after a long pause.

"You're right, Kirk, you're the man to do it. I could hire any one else for the job, but you've a reason of your own for wanting Allen dead. When you get Allen, you can collect the rewards on his head by dragging his carcass over into the next State. In addition, I'll pay you a thousand dollars."

"A thousand ain't enough," Dixie Kirk answered. "It's got to be more."

They fell to haggling over the price to be paid for a human life as coldly as though they were appraising a piece of furniture. Finally Captain Painton agreed to pay Dixie Kirk two thousand dollars for the killing of Jim-twin Allen.

"But you can't wait to do it," Captain Painton declared grimly. "If he has told the truth—if he knows who I am, and where my hide-out is—he can't die too soon. By the way, have you ever run up agin' Allen before?"

"Yeah," Kirk drawled. "Years ago. He tried to get me for a little rustlin' job. I would've got hung, if a couple of friends of mine hadn't got me out of the lockup in time, after Allen was gone. An' I never was in want fer a little dinero when Cyrus Thompson was alive. Allen got him. That's another reason I got for wantin' to fill him full of lead."

Captain Painton was staring at Kirk fixedly. "You understand that I've tried to get Allen killed before; but I've failed. I have not tried to do it myself because I am not a gunman. I hire men to do my fighting. But up until now Allen hasn't been touched. I'm at the end of my patience. I have met with nothing but failure in trying to get Allen, but now there is no time to waste.

"Allen and I are facing the end. Either he must go, or I do. I intend that he shall be the one to die. Kirk, you've got the job of killing him. If you fail, you alone will be responsible. And if you fail, Kirk, you'll pay for your failure with your life."

"It looks like I've got to get Allen, or we'll both get it," Kirk remarked slowly.

"That's the size of it. Now get out of here, Kirk. And don't come back until you bring me the news that Allen is dead."

"You won't see me again till Allen is playin' a harp," Kirk answered grimly, as he turned and pushed through the door of the cabin.

Through the partly opened door, Captain Painton watched Dixie Kirk disappear in the darkness. He turned back and strode to the table with quick, angry steps. Suddenly he crashed his fist to the table top and blurted:

"Allen must die! This time he's got to die."

THE LEGION PLANS A FIGHT

ALLEN LOOKED MORE THAN EVER LIKE AN IRRESPONSIBLE kid as he walked down the main street of Carson carrying a fresh apple pie in his hands. When he reached the Ranger headquarters, he hurried to the open space in the rear. His two grays, Princess and Honey Boy, were there, and as soon as they saw him coming with the pie they whinnied joyfully.

Allen grinned broadly as he broke off big pieces of the stuff and fed it to the two grays. Princess and Honey Boy tossed their heads and flashed their teeth as they snatched it out of his fingers.

When the pasty was gone, he licked his sticky fingers, then patted the grays' necks and rubbed their muzzles.

These two horses meant the world to him. More than once they had saved him from death and capture. With a last pat, he left them and walked around to the front entrance of the Ranger headquarters, his face still split by a broad grin.

As Allen went inside, King, his big wolf dog, came from a corner toward him. He stopped and ruffled King's shaggy hair, talking to him in a low, crooning tone. The big dog whimpered and growled softly in greeting.

"Sounds just like you two was talkin' together," Doc Candee remarked from the bunk in the corner, on which he was lying. "I know King would never hurt me because I'm your friend, but sometimes when I look at those fangs and yellow eyes of his, I can't help shiverin'."

"Shucks, King wouldn't hurt a baby," Allen answered.

"Nope, he wouldn't, but he'd sure tear the throat out of a two-legged skunk if he got the chance," Candee retorted.

"How are you feelin' now, Doc?" Allen inquired.

"I'm gettin' my strength back fast. It won't be long now afore I'm up and around again. Gosh, you make me feel like an old woman, forcin' me to stay in bed just because I got winged."

Yeah, but I'm goin' to need you soon, and I want you to mend as soon as possible," Allen answered.

Suddenly a call came from outside. Allen stepped through the open door and looked upward. "Tiny Tim" Murphy, a little good-natured man with an Irish face, was on duty in the lookout tower. He was one of the few regular Rangers detailed under Allen's command, and he worshiped his captain as a sort of god.

84

"Jim, there's a rider headin' this way, and it looks like Captain Harrison," he called down excitedly.

"Yeah, I've been expectin' him," Allen answered.

Allen stepped out into the street and saw immediately that the man riding toward Carson was, in truth, Captain Harry Harrison. Harrison was State chief of the Rangers and had been instrumental in drafting Allen to the service of the law. Allen waited at the hitch rack until Harrison rode up and dismounted.

He was over fifty, a grizzled old-timer. He had faded blue eyes and a tanned face as dark as old leather. Though he looked grim and merciless, he was known for his sense of fair play and honesty. He strode forward and gripped Allen's hand warmly.

"I thought I better be ridin' down here to see you, Jim, since I got your letter askin' if I could send you more regular Rangers," he said.

"Yeah, I thought you'd come," Allen answered with a grin. "You must have a feelin' that things are goin' to begin happenin' and you don't want to miss the fun."

"Not much, I don't. You've got a reason for askin' for more men to add to your Legion. I want to find out what it is," Harrison remarked.

"Shucks, I've just got a hunch that I'm goin' to need 'em to fight the gang. Are they comin'?"

Captain Harrison's face clouded. "Jim, you asked me for men at a bad time. I just sent some Rangers up north to look into some cattle rustlin', and I had to send another detachment over to Midas to guard a gold mine that's in danger because of a strike. The rest of them have got their regular duties and can't be called away except in an emergency. Even if you come to need 'em that bad, I won't be able to call 'em until later."

"Gosh, then it'll be too late. I reckon it's goin' to be up to the Legion."

"You mean you're plannin' an attack?"

"Yeah. It's goin' to be a last stand between the gang and the Legion. Either Captain Painton's men or my men is goin' to be wiped out."

"I know better'n to ask you questions, Jim. You wouldn't tell me anything anyway. You're in charge here, and fightin' the gang is strickly up to you. You know you can count on me for all the help I can give you."

"Sure, I know that," Allen answered slowly.

"Looks like the whole government of the State is movin' down this way for a while," Captain Harrison went on with a smile. "Amos Stringer, his wife, and daughter left the capitol afore I did, headin' for the Circle G Ranch. The Circle G is run by Mrs. Stringer's brother, Jeff Gordon, and she's payin' him a visit. Then the governor said somethin' abut comin' down here, too."

Allen nodded. Amos Stringer was the attorney general of the State. The governor was "Big Bill" Harrison, Captain Harry's brother. These three men had formed the committee which had issued the call for Allen to side with the law.

"Stringer says he wants to see you, so I reckon you better be runnin' over to the Circle G soon," Harrison suggested.

"Yeah, and I want to see Stringer," Allen answered. "He's been holdin' us down pretty strict, but I reckon when the fun starts the Legion ain't goin' to worry much about doin' things legal."

"I reckon you'd better argue that out with Stringer," Captain Harrison said with a smile. "I'm too tired to talk about it now."

Harrison turned to walk into the headquarters building. Allen paused, however, and looked across the road at a man who was just dismounting in front of the general store. His grin faded and he stood motionless. He recognized Dixie Kirk. His face did not change expression as Kirk walked toward him.

" 'Lo, Dixie," Allen said softly.

" 'Lo, Allen. I reckon you're surprised to see me. The last you knew of me, a sheriff was gettin' a noose ready to put around my neck."

"Yeah, but I heard you got loose again. What you comin' around here for, Dixie?"

"I come to see you, Allen. I don't hold nothin' agin' you for ropin' me that time and turnin' me over to the sheriff. I'm hopin' we can let bygones be bygones."

"When I roped you it wasn't because I had anything personal agin' you, Dixie," Jim Allen answered. "There was an innocent man who was goin' to be hung for the rustlin', and the only way I could save him was to get the real rustlers. So long as Hank Martin wasn't strung up for somethin' he never did, I'm sort of glad you got loose afterward."

"Yeah, after all we're both long riders," Dixie Kirk answered slyly. "Now I've come here hopin' to hitch up with you and the Legion."

Allen looked surprised. "You want to join the Legion? What for?"

"Because you're fightin' the dope-runnin' gang. I want to help you. I reckon you never knew I had a kid brother. Well, a little while ago I found out the kid was usin' dope. I couldn't make him stop. The kid sort of went crazy from the stuff, got into a gun fight, and was killed. I figured that the dope-runnin' gang is responsible for his death, so I'm aimin' to get back at 'em."

For a moment Allen said nothing. Dixie Kirk looked into Allen's strange eyes and shivered. It seemed to him that Allen was looking straight through him, reading his thoughts. For a moment he was filled with panic, fearful that Allen knew he was lying.

He was vastly relieved when at last Allen answered:

"I sure sympathize with you, Dixie. I'm glad you come along. It'll help to have you with us."

"I'd sure consider it an honor to belong to the Outlaw Legion," Kirk declared with simulated enthusiasm.

"Then you come on in and I'll have Captain Harrison administer the oath," Allen suggested.

As Allen turned away, Dixie Kirk's mouth curved slightly in a hard, satisfied grin.

Kirk's confidence was immediately shattered, however, when he entered the front office.

King rose quickly from his position beside Doc Candee's bunk. He bared his sharp fangs and growled threateningly. Dixie Kirk stopped short, his face a picture of fear. Instinctively he reached for his gun.

"King! Stay back! What's the matter with you, anyway, old fellow? Don't you know Dixie Kirk's a friend of ours?" asked Allen.

King immediately backed away. His animosity seemed to vanish immediately, though he still kept his yellow eyes turned on Kirk. Kirk laughed nervously.

"Gosh, I didn't know what was goin' to happen then, Allen," he exclaimed breathlessly.

"Shucks, King's just gettin' old and he feels mean sometimes," Allen answered with a grin. "You go over and pat him. He'll be all right."

Dixie Kirk looked startled at the invitation, but he realized that unless he complied, Allen might suspect him. He crossed the room warily. King remained motionless as

Kirk reached down to stroke him, but a threatening growl came from his throat. Another sharp command from Allen silenced him. After a moment Dixie Kirk was only too glad to back away from the dog.

"Now I reckon you two are friends," Allen remarked casually.

Turning, he explained to Harrison that Kirk was seeking membership in the Outlaw Legion. Kirk said nothing until Allen finished, then he remarked:

"I sure won't rest till I've done my part to wipe out the dope-runnin' gang. If I can't do it with the Legion, then I'll fight the gang alone."

"That's talkin'," Captain Harrison remarked approvingly. "Jim's recommendation is good enough for me. We won't waste any time about it, Kirk. We'll swear you in right now."

Captain Harrison proceeded to administer the oath to Dixie Kirk. Kirk appeared to be listening solemnly, but he was inwardly laughing at the ease with which he had deceived every one. At the completion of the little ceremony, he shook hands with Captain Harrison and Allen, and was introduced to Doc Candee.

"Now I'm ready for orders," he announced.

"I reckon there won't be any for a while," Allen answered. "It'll be better if nobody else knows you've joined the Legion. You just wander around like you wasn't doin' anything. When the proper times comes, I'll send you word."

"That suits me. I'm hungry, and I'm goin' out to get somethin' to eat," Kirk said.

With a wave of the hand he stepped outside and walked down the street.

"Gosh, Jim, I can't figure why you let that gent join up," Doc exclaimed, rising on his elbow in his bunk.

"He looks mean as a killer mule. I don't trust him. King don't like him, either, and that ought to be warnin' enough."

"Shucks, what reason have you got for dislikin' him, Doc?" Allen asked innocently.

"None, but I'm suspicious of him all the same. He's a killer. Bein' in with the Legion, he'll be able to keep an eye on you and maybe plug you in the back sometime when you ain't lookin' for it."

"Gosh, you sure think murderous thoughts, Doc." Allen grinned. "I don't hardly think Dixie Kirk would do a thing like that. On the other hand, suppose you're right. Why, then, if he come here to watch me close by gettin' in the Legion, it works the other way around. Havin' him one of us, I can watch him close, too."

"Then you do think he might try it?" Doc Candee exclaimed. "You deliberately let him join up with us when you think he's here to kill you!"

"I never said that. I was only supposin'," Allen answered softly.

"Yeah, but you're figurin' somethin' yourself, you contrary little cuss," Doc declared. "Your trail is sure hard to follow. Sometimes I think I'm way ahead of you, then find out you're a dozen thinks ahead of me all the time. You're plannin' somethin' right now, Jim, and I know it."

"Sure," Allen answered with a wide grin. "I'm plannin' to ride over to the Circle G and have a talk with Amos Stringer."

"Now you listen here; I want to know this straight," Doc Candee protested. "Do you suspect Dixie Kirk or don't you?"

"Shucks, I always give the other gent the benefit of the doubt," was all the answer Allen would make.

"You aggravatin' hombre!" Candee exploded. "You don't tell nobody nothin'!"

"I tell you one thing, Doc. It ain't goin' to be long now afore Captain Painton and me face each other and shoot it out," Allen said softly.

Before any one could speak another word to him, he hurried around to the rear of the building. The next moment he was riding quickly out of Carson, his legs dangling loosely in Indian fashion.

"Gosh, old lady, Captain Painton and me are sure settlin' down to a battle of wits," he remarked grimly to Princess. "Maybe I've got the edge on him so far, and maybe I ain't. But an old professor told me once about a thing called psychology: which means that if you do what the other gent ain't expectin', you got this psychology workin' for you, and it's darned strong medicine."

Princess twitched her ears as though she understood perfectly, and galloped on.

THE NIGHT ATTACK

AT NOON ALLEN RODE THROUGH THE GATE OF THE Circle G Ranch, which was located about twelve miles from Carson, near Strawberry Creek. As he jogged toward the house, which was on a rise overlooking the spread of range land, he saw four persons sitting on the porch. He recognized Amos Stringer, the attorney general, and Jeff Gordon, the owner of the outfit. There was an elderly woman sitting in a rocker, and a girl near her, whom Allen had never seen before.

" 'Lo, Mr. Stringer. 'Lo, Jeff," he shouted as he rode near.

"If it ain't Jim Allen!" Jeff Gordon boomed. "We were just talkin' about you, Jim."

He was a big, jovial man, with a smile like a beaming sun. He gripped Allen's hand in a powerful hand. Then Allen turned and shook hands with Amos Stringer, who was as reserved and cool as Jeff Gordon was friendly.

"I heard you wanted to talk with me, so I come over, Mr. Stringer," Allen remarked. "I've been wantin' to settle some matters with you myself."

"Glad you came, Allen," Stringer answered. "We just arrived a little while ago. Maybe you know that Jeff is my brother-in-law. I'd like you to meet Mrs. Stringer and my daughter."

Allen was always bashful in the presence of women, and he did not stir until Jeff Gordon grasped his arm and drew him forward. Mrs. Stringer was looking at him eagerly and holding out her hand. She did not wait for an introduction, but burst out:

"You're Jim Allen? Why, I never was so surprised. I thought you would be a big, hard-looking man. But I know all the wonderful things you've done. I'm so happy to meet you, and I'm proud to shake your hand."

Allen was so confused and embarrassed that he could hardly mumble an answer. He felt immediately the warmth and kindliness of Mrs. Stringer's nature.

She was a stately woman, with a finely molded face, and though her hair was silver, there was a dancing youthfulness in her eyes. Then Allen noticed a pair of crutches leaning against her chair, and he realized that she was a cripple. He almost forgot his own uneasiness in his solicitation for her.

"Shucks, I ain't done much," he answered. "You're just bein' kind to me."

"But we were only just talking about how you've

92

stepped in and stopped Cyrus Thompson's rule along the border. And now you're fighting the dope-running gang," Mrs. Stringer persisted. "You've done what nobody else has been able to do. You've done the State more good than all the regular law officers; yet every one calls you 'Wolf.' If you're a wolf, then I wish there were more like you."

"Gosh, I don't deserve havin' nice things like that said about me," Allen protested.

"You deserve far more. One reason why I wanted to come and visit Jeff was the chance of meeting you, Jim Allen. That's enough reason for the long journey down here."

Mrs. Stringer then introduced Allen to her daughter, Nora, who had come forward and displayed a frank, open interest. She clasped Allen's hand firmly, in a manner that made Allen warm to her immediately. Here was a girl who was sure of herself, courageous and fine.

"I'm happy to know you, too, Mr. Allen," she said.

Allen talked with them a few moments, then noticed that Amos Stringer was becoming impatient. After a while Stringer suggested that his wife had better go inside and rest from her journey.

Mrs. Stringer agreed, and her husband helped her from her chair. It hurt Allen to see her adjust her crutches and limp into the house. Every move must cause her pain, but not a complaint came from her.

Allen was impressed by the change that came over Amos Stringer when he gave his attention to his wife. Usually he was surly and impatient, but now he was all consideration. He helped Mrs. Stringer into the house with the utmost care. His face softened, and Allen realized now how much Amos loved his wife.

While they were inside the house, Allen remarked gently to Jeff Gordon:

"It's sure too bad she's lame. She's one of the finest women I ever met."

"It's a pity," Gordon answered soberly. "It happened only about five years ago. At that time Amos was sheriff up in Nodaway County. There were some killin's up there, all done by rustlers. Amos finally arrested the man he knew was the leader of the rustlers, a man named Crossman. Crossman was put into the lockup.

"But the people were crazy to get at Crossman. They were all respectable folks, but they were so het up agin' him that they didn't know what they were doin'. The mob was loco. They never stopped to think. They started stormin' the jail, tryin' to get Amos to let Crossman out, and Amos was tryin' to hold 'em off. While this was goin' on, Charlotte—Mrs. Stringer—happened to come down the street toward the jail. When the crowd saw her, they let out a shout and started for her.

"There was no sense to what they did, but they were all out of their senses. They grabbed Charlotte and hollered that Crossman should be let out. Before anybody knew what was happening, she was thrown under the buggy she come in. Then the horses got scared and reared, and started to run off. She was badly trampled. For a while everybody thought she was dead. The mob quieted down right away, but it was too late then. Ever since, Charlotte has been a cripple. It would have made most other women sour on life, but she's never complained. She just says they didn't know what they was doin'."

"It's a wonder Stringer didn't shoot that mob down," Allen said in a hard, flat tone.

94

"I reckon he was too concerned about her to think of that. But it's changed him, all right," Jeff Gordon went on. "It turned him bitter and nervous. He tried to get the ones that did it, but he never could. But ever since then he's cared for Charlotte every day of her life. He sure loves her, and Nora, too."

"And I reckon they look up to him," Allen said soberly.

"They couldn't get along without him," Jeff Gordon agreed.

"Gosh, it sort of gets me to think about it," Allen declared.

At that moment Amos Stringer came out of the house. Again he was the irritable man he usually was.

"What do you want to see me about, Allen?" he asked nervously.

"About bein' a wolf," Allen answered cryptically.

"What? What do you mean?" Stringer snapped.

"I sure get tired of bein' called the Wolf, but I reckon that's what I am," Allen explained sadly. "And I reckon my Legion is all wolves, too. We come here and promised to clean up the dope-runnin' gang, and we've been doin' it. But the time has come when we can't fight accordin' to the law any more."

"I've already warned you about that, Allen," Stringer objected. "Your job is to make arrests."

"My job is to clean up the gang," Allen differed sharply. "I've been tryin' to do things legal-like to please you, but she can't be did any more. Captain Painton fights us any way he can. We've got to get him with his own weapons. If we don't do that, we'll never get him."

Stringer's face turned an angry red. "I've warned you, Allen. You can't fly in the face of the law. If you can't handle the gang in a legal manner, you'll

95

answer for it. There can't be any other way."

"There is one other way, and that's the wolf's way," Allen retorted.

"Are you defying me?" Stringer demanded as he rose angrily from his chair.

"Nope. I'm only tellin' you that, warnin' or no warnin', from now on me and my pack of wolves is fightin' their own way. We're facin' a show-down with Captain Painton, and we ain't goin' to take no chance of losin' him."

"You disregard my orders, and I'll disband the Legion and run you out of the State, Allen," Stringer almost shouted.

Allen looked intently at Stringer. The attorney general stood his ground for a moment, then wilted. He sank back into his chair and sighed.

"I shouldn't 've said that, Allen. You've already done so much that it would be rank ingratitude to turn against you now. Only, I am not the only one concerned. There is the public to consider. I am only a servant of the people of this State. If you start killing again, they will rise up and shout for your pelt. Then I won't have any choice but to do as they demand. Remember, you're in a dangerous position here. You're free on bail, on a charge of murder, and at any time we might be forced to call you to trial. If that happens, you'll surely be convicted and sentenced to hanging."

"Why, Amos, the governor would pardon him the minute the sentence was passed," Jeff Gordon protested.

"Perhaps so, and perhaps not," Stringer answered. "The governor is a servant of the people, the same as I am. Sometimes we can't do as we like to, personally; we have to do what is demanded of us."

"That sure sounds hard on you, Allen," Jeff Gordon remarked ruefully.

"Shucks, I ain't worryin' about what might happen to me," Allen answered. "I've been dodgin' the law for fourteen years and I'm used to it. Only, I ain't goin' to leave here till I've got Captain Painton and cleaned out the gang. I made that promise, and I'm goin' to stick to it whether I'm with the written law or agin' it.

"Just because somethin' is written in a book, that don't make it law," Allen continued slowly. "The thing that's right is the law, and everybody knows that. The worst of doin' things lawful is that it wastes time and maybe fails altogether—guilty men go free."

"I guess there's no use arguing with you, Allen," Stringer said shortly.

"Nope," Allen said stubbornly. "I'm goin' to get Captain Painton in my own way, no matter what is done to me afterward."

"Allen, have you any idea who Captain Painton really is?" Stringer asked him suddenly.

"Wolves know lots of things, and they don't talk much. They've got funny ways of figurin' things," Allen retorted, and then rode off before Stringer could press him for a more definite answer.

Jim Allen returned to Carson late in the afternoon. He left Princess at the hitch rack in front of the Ranger headquarters and walked inside. He was delighted to find Toothpick Jarrick there with "Bad Bill" Rodgers and Dixie Kirk.

"We been waitin' for you, Jim," Toothpick called out excitedly. "We know you've got somethin' on your mind and we want to know what it is."

"You're right. The time's come to tell you about it,"

Allen answered. "I've found out that Captain Painton and his gang is goin' to hold a meetin' tonight, and I'm figurin' that the Outlaw Legion is goin' to round 'em up."

Toothpick gasped. "How'd you find that out, Jim?" he asked quickly.

"Early this mornin' I went up to the ledge where we had the fight last night. Mace Dodge was still lyin' there. I give him a decent burial, but I looked through his pockets first to see what I could find. He had a note on him, signed with the initials 'C. P.', which means Captain Painton. The note said that a meetin' is called tonight at midnight, out at Nine Mile Camp."

"Gosh, then we've got a chance of gettin' the gang wholesale, and grabbin' Captain Painton, too," Toothpick cried.

"Yeah, but we got to go at it careful. Toothpick, you and Bad Bill, and Dixie Kirk ride out to Mesa Verde and get the Legion prepared. Don't tell 'em what we're goin' to do, but just warn 'em to get ready. You better start right away."

"Gosh, we've been itchin' for another chance to fight the gang; now we've got it!" Toothpick ejaculated.

Dixie Kirk pretended to be as overjoyed as the others, but in reality he was startled and apprehensive.

He knew of the meeting called for Nine Mile Camp; in fact, he and Mace Dodge had been spreading the news and moving south toward the meeting place for the purpose of attending.

He realized immediately that Captain Painton should be warned at all costs, and that no one could do it but him. He cast about desperately for some means of getting the news to the gang leader, but before he could reach a decision, Toothpick Jarrick seized his arm and exclaimed:

"Come on, we got to be goin'."

Dixie Kirk followed Toothpick and Bad Bill Rogers out of the building to the hitch rack. As they mounted their horses, he held back, still trying to think of a way out of his predicament. Suddenly he said:

"Wait a minute. I've got to get me some more cartridges afore I leave town."

His plan was to slip into the general store, then out the back, and into the offices of the Carson *Clarion,* published by Ed Blendine, who was almost as powerful in the gang as Captain Painton. Blendine would be able to relay the important information to Painton. No sooner had Dixie Kirk decided upon this move, however, than Toothpick blocked his way.

"No, you don't need to buy any bullets. The Legion's got plenty. We'll give you all you need. Come on, you ride along with us, and don't waste a minute. We ain't got any time to lose."

Dixie Kirk had no choice but to do as Toothpick Jarrick ordered. To insist on his object would arouse Toothpick's suspicions. He did not argue, but climbed into his saddle. Immediately the three of them started off, riding at top speed. Toothpick led the way, and Dixie Kirk brought up the rear.

Kirk then decided that he would grasp his chance and slip off the trail while Toothpick and Bad Bill were not watching, then hurry back to Carson and warn Ed Blendine.

Kirk allowed Toothpick and Bad Bill to gain on him. They were riding through hilly country now. Within a few minutes, Kirk saw his chance, when they reached a bend in the trail which was bordered by a thick growth of saplings. He stopped quietly, turned his horse, and began to cut away while the others moved on, out of sight. But when he barely got his pony off the trail, he heard Toothpick call:

"Come on, Kirk. Stick close to us, it's gettin' dark and you don't know the way."

Dixie Kirk cursed under his breath. He was obliged to abandon his second plan. There was no hope now that he would be able to warn Captain Painton.

Then it occurred to him that during the attack on the gang meeting there would be a general mix-up and much confusion. He would have an excellent opportunity to put a bullet into Jim Allen's back. He could not have wished for anything better.

ALLEN RETURNS

MESA VERDE WAS A BROAD SPREAD OF VERDANT, rolling country. Months ago the Outlaw Legion had established camp on it, in a bend of the Dirty Devil Creek. Allen's object in removing the Legion from Carson was to make it impossible for the gang to spy upon them and learn their moves.

When Toothpick Jarrick, Bad Bill Rogers, and Dixie Kirk rode into the camp with the news sent by Allen, there was general excitement.

Though these men were hardened outlaws, they behaved like a bunch of schoolboys granted an unexpected holiday, flinging their hats in the air and cheering. Then they went about the business of preparing themselves for the attack on the gang. It grew late and, when Allen did not appear, they became impatient.

"Where's Jim?" Pat Garrett, the Arizona ex-sheriff demanded of Toothpick Jarrick. "He ought to be here by now."

"Gosh, the little devil's like a flea; nobody ever knows when or where he's goin' to pop up next," Toothpick answered.

"Can't you tell us where we're goin' to go?" asked the Yuma Kid.

"Nope. Jim'll tell you that hisself. You know what a cautious little cuss he is," Bad Bill answered.

Dixie Kirk had been introduced to the members of the Legion. They welcomed him with apparent friendliness, but he thought he detected a bit of wariness in their manner. This made him conduct himself very carefully, lest he betray himself.

A camp fire blazed near the bank of the creek and the men gathered around it. Now and then they looked across the dark mesa in the hope of seeing Allen. Toothpick remained alert, ready to give the word when Allen appeared. He walked out into the darkness, peered all around, then came back disappointedly.

"He ain't anywhere near yet," he announced.

A few seconds later, however, Allen appeared in the glow of light around the fire. Grinning broadly, he slipped off Princess and mingled with the men. They slapped his back in an enthusiastic welcome.

"Gosh, Jim, where'd you come from? You wasn't out there a minute ago," Toothpick Jarrick gasped.

"Shucks, I was ridin' right at you then. I seen you lookin' for me," Allen answered with a chuckle.

"Gosh," Toothpick blurted, "I'd sure hate to have you trailin' me. It would be like bein' haunted."

Allen laughed and quickly checked up on the members of the Legion gathered around him. Besides the Yuma Kid and Pat Garrett, there were the Cole brothers, Tom and George, who were wanted in Kansas; Frank Mills, the Panhandle outlaw; "Silent Sam" Henry, who, though he was owner of the Snaffle Bit Ranch, was always ready to aid the Legion; and "Hasty Hugh" Higgins, operator of the Wrench Ranch, whose friendship Allen had won by saving him from being preyed upon by rustlers.

There were also half a dozen others, all outlaws and wanted in several States, who were ready to follow Allen anywhere.

"Jim, we're ready to ride with you when you say the word," Tom Cole exclaimed eagerly.

"Then listen to me a minute," Allen remarked, and at his words the men grew quiet. "We're headin' for Nine Mile Camp, where the gang is holdin' a meetin' tonight. It's a council of war, and they're goin' to decide on how they're goin' to fight us next. I reckon Captain Painton is goin' to be there. If he is, it's goin' to be my job to capture him."

"If we see him, we'll all head for the hombre," Frank Mills exclaimed. "What's he look like, Jim?"

Allen was the only member of the Outlaw Legion who had ever seen Captain Painton. He took advantage of this fact when he answered:

"Nope, I ain't goin' to tell you what he looks like. I'm aimin' to rope him myself. You men keep the gang busy. I'll make a rush for Captain Painton when I see him. Now, listen careful. We'll go at 'em like a pack of timber wolves, meanin' we'll circle 'em, then draw in closer, so none of 'em can break away. I'll give the signal. Start closin' in when you hear my wolf call.

"Nine Mile Camp is on the other side of the Marching Men Hills," Allen continued in a hard, flat tone. "We'll ride together till we get to the hills, then we'll split. Half of you go through Tank Canyon, and the other half through Dog Canyon, with me. Go careful when you come out on the other side, then begin circlin'. When you hear my wolf call, you start ridin' and shootin' for all you're worth. Now we better be goin'."

The men silently left the camp fire and sought their horses. Allen ordered Toothpick to lead the other detachment through Tank Canyon when they reached the Marching Men Hills. He would lead the other. Toothpick regretted that he must be separated from Allen, but he agreed.

Bad Bill Rogers rode by Allen's side as they began to move off, and Dixie Kirk kept close behind Princess.

"When it's over, head back for our camp, and bring your prisoners with you," Allen called as a last command. "Wait here till I show up."

"Yeah, but you ain't ever goin' to show up here again," Dixie Kirk vowed under his breath as he watched Allen closely.

The band of riders moved quietly through the darkness. Every man was grimly intent on what lay ahead. Each knew that the coming fight would bring death to some of their number, but that was to be expected. Allen had risked his life again and again while fighting the dope-running gang; the least any of them could do was follow him.

It was past midnight and the gang meeting was probably in progress. Captain Painton had chosen an excellent spot for the meeting. Nine Mile Camp was an abandoned town, consisting of a few deserted ramshackle structures.

It was in the open and there were many old trails connecting with it. Even if they were all blocked by Allen's men, it might be possible for the gang to retreat into the hills behind the town, where pursuit would be difficult and places of hiding many.

103

Allen realized this and intended to attack the town from the direction of the hills while Toothpick's detachment approached from the other side. Even so, the gang was almost sure to outnumber the Legion by two to one.

At last the riding Legion reached the base of the Marching Men Hills. There, at a word from Allen, they separated into two parties. Toothpick Jarrick led his bunch slightly northward, toward the entrance of Tank Canyon, while Allen turned south.

Allen led the way for his men, with Bad Bill Rogers riding beside him, and Dixie Kirk behind.

To the rear of Kirk the others followed. Kirk knew that he would have no opportunity to fire at Allen until the attack began and they scattered. When he found Allen cut off from the others, his chance would come.

He was already counting the thousands of dollars reward he could collect when he turned the White Wolf's dead body over to the sheriff of the first county across the State line.

Tonight the thin shell of a new moon hung in the sky, and threw a dim glow into Dog Canyon. Allen led his men through it carefully and slowly. He did not know where the gang might have posted sentries, who might detect his coming and warn the meeting.

Once they were out of the canyon, the going was easier. Flat ground lay ahead, baked as hard as brick. Nine Mile Camp lay straight ahead, in a hollow.

Allen peered into the distance and detected a faint glow which only a camp fire could make. The fire itself was hidden by the shacks of the town, but Allen's heart leaped because he knew that the gang must be gathered around it.

Within a mile of the meeting place, Allen made a

silent signal. His men stopped and gathered around him. Speaking in a whisper so low that it was almost inaudible, he ordered:

"Begin spreadin' out, right and left. Leave about a hundred yards between you, then wait. Toothpick's got farther to travel, so we'll give him some more time before we let loose. Listen for my wolf call."

His men obeyed immediately. They moved away silently, spreading out in a line on both sides. Bad Bill Rogers stationed himself on the right of Allen, while Dixie Kirk took a position on Allen's left. Kirk's thin lips pressed tightly together, and his muscles grew tense, as he realized that his moment was coming. He was right-handed, and his position on Allen's left was perfect for his purpose. He itched to fire at Allen, but he forced himself to wait.

Then, suddenly, the signal came. Just before the uncanny howl made the air tremble, Bad Bill Rogers realized Allen had heard something that told him Toothpick Jarrick was now in position. The sound came from Allen's throat, a long, wailing, mournful note such as that uttered by the lobo wolf. Then the next instant Allen was rushing toward the ghost town with the swiftness of the wind.

Every man in the line went into action. They rode at top speed, all centering on Nine Mile Camp. As they came closer, the glow of the camp fire among the buildings grew brighter. Dixie Kirk was taken by surprise at Allen's sudden move. Allen seemed to disappear completely in the darkness. Kirk spurted ahead, hunting for him, but without avail. Princess was running so quietly, and the other horses were making such a noise, that Kirk was bewildered. He jerked out his gun and held it ready for the moment when he would glimpse Allen again.

On the other side of town, Toothpick Jarrick heard the wild cry of the wolf. The instant it reached his ears he and his men began charging toward Nine Mile Camp. The riders of the Outlaw Legion had now formed a great circle which was contracting and drawing toward the town in the center.

In Nine Mile Camp the members of the dope-running gang stood in a circle around the camp fire. All of them were hard, tough-looking men. They numbered more than two score, and represented the men who were in charge of the various operations and distributing stations of the gang under Captain Painton.

Captain Painton himself was in the center of the group, talking to them in his harsh, cold voice, when the uncanny wolf call reached his ears.

He stopped speaking abruptly and stared around. The sound made every man there jerk his hands toward his guns. They stood as still as statues, listening. Then, on the wind, came the sound of running horses. Captain Painton was the first to recover.

"Get out of town," he shouted wildly. "It's Allen's men, and they're closin' in. Scatter and stop 'em!"

The cry was enough to make a bedlam out of the meeting. The men, shouting and cursing, dashed for their horses. One or two lingered, looking at Captain Painton curiously. They saw him duck out of sight between two of the buildings. Then concern for their own safety overcame them, and they sped out of the circle of light with the others. In a moment the camp fire was deserted.

"Come on, wolves!" Toothpick Jarrick shouted shrilly.

It was the battle cry of the Legion. From the first it

had rallied them against the forces of the gang. It seemed to have a magical effect on Allen's men. They spurred their horses and rushed ahead more rapidly, their guns drawn and ready for action. Then the cry was echoed by others until it seemed that a whole army was closing in around Nine Mile Camp.

"Come on, wolves!"

The dope-running gang opened fire first. Rattling gunfire came from the shacks. The Outlaw Legion answered with swift bullets.

At the first report, pandemonium broke loose. The members of the dope-running gang, finding themselves surrounded, began to fight with frenzied desperation. The Outlaw Legion, realizing that everything depended upon their keeping the gang inside the moving circle, answered with a savage gun attack.

Dixie Kirk raced right and left, swearing savagely and swinging his Colts, still searching for Allen. He had not sighted Allen for even a split second after the wolf call had urged the Legion into action.

Now he found himself in a dangerous position. He might be fired upon and killed by other members of the gang. Realizing this he was forced to keep out of the way by dodging behind the other members of the Legion. He continued to look for Allen as best he could, but still without success.

The attacking dope runners now rushed madly toward the circle of Legion riders in an attempt to break through. The result was even faster shooting and wilder confusion. Allen's men massed toward the center of the attack, hoping to stem the tide of riders.

For a few moments they churned and mixed so that one could not tell friend from foe. In bewilderment they were forced to stop firing, but that was the chance,

Captain Painton's men were looking for. Before the Legion riders could stop them, they had broken through and were dashing away.

Toothpick kept shouting like a Sioux warrior as he urged his men on. Finding the ground ahead of him clear, he galloped for the center of the town. Brandishing his gun, he sped down the street, whooping at the top of his lungs.

Suddenly he felt a bullet whistle past his head, and jerked around just in time to see one of the dope runners crouching behind a corner of the shack. The man's horse had been killed and he had run back for shelter.

Toothpick answered with his Colts and the man sprawled out on the ground, a bullet between the eyes.

Toothpick's left arm was wet with blood from a flesh wound in his shoulder, but he did not even notice it. He continued his rush through the town. Even above the clatter of gunfire his sharp cry could be heard:

"Come on, wolves!"

The Yuma Kid was riding desperately away after the gang. A bullet had pierced his hat and furrowed across the top of his head, and the flow of blood was running down across his face and almost blinding him. He was speeding past a clump of trees when an unexpected burst of fire came from behind them.

The bullets hit the Yuma Kid and with a hoarse shout he fell out of his saddle. Stunned and wounded as he was, he managed to drag himself up. He glimpsed a dark movement behind the trees and fired swiftly. A howl of pain resulted.

Again the Yuma Kid fired, then fell to his knees, too weak to hold himself up. As he sprawled out on the ground, he fired again. A tight grin formed on his lips when he saw one of the dope-running gang leap away from the tree in a spasm of pain and fall limply to the ground. Then the gun fell from the Yuma Kid's hand, and blackness closed over him.

"Come on, wolves!"

He tried to shout the words, but they were only a whisper. Then his body quivered and he died.

Dixie Kirk was half crazy with anxiety. He was in extreme danger of being killed by one of his own gang. As best he could he kept away from the hottest of the fight and searched for Allen, who continued to remain missing.

Pat Garrett sped alongside the shacks of the town, keeping in the shadows. As he passed each space between the structures he fired into it. His first bullet dropped a dope runner who was huddling there and waiting for a Legion man to come riding through the street. His next, sent two more rushing into the open.

Garrett sped after them and dropped them with two well-placed bullets. Howling in triumph, he circled, reloaded his gun, and began driving others of the gang from their hiding places in the deserted town.

Those who had happened to see the deaths of the first three men Garrett had routed out began to shout their surrender. They came trotting into the open with their hands raised.

Garrett rode around them swiftly, swearing to kill any of them that dropped his hands. They submitted meekly. The Arizona ex-sheriff found himself with three prisoners on his hands, which he had taken without help.

The fight around Nine Mile Camp seemed to end almost as quickly as it had begun. Many of the gang had escaped or been killed. Almost all of them were out of ammunition and could no longer fight. The Outlaw

Legion had had the advantage of surprise on their side and had suffered fewer casualties. Enough of Allen's men were left to surround the prisoners. Gradually the firing ceased.

Then Toothpick Jarrick's voice called ringingly:

"Head back for the mesa."

The men responded slowly. They sensed that their attack had not been entirely successful, and they were unwilling to call it quits; but there was nothing else they could do.

They banded together, keeping their prisoners in the center of a circle of riders. Toothpick Jarrick rode swiftly around the town. He saw Dixie Kirk also on the search, and ordered Kirk to help take care of the captives. Then Toothpick called:

"Jim! Jim Allen!"

He received no answer. He was on the point of continuing his search for his captain when he remembered that Allen's orders were to the effect that the Legion was to wait for him at the camp on Mesa Verde.

Toothpick turned back doubtfully and joined the group moving away from Nine Mile. It was only then that he realized he was wounded. A hard chuckle came from his throat and he forgot about his injury almost at once.

At the camp on Mesa Verde the Legion came together again, a grim, silent group of men. Toothpick Jarrick and Bad Bill Rogers paced about, waiting impatiently for Allen's return. They would not even care for their wounds until their captain returned.

They said nothing, not daring to voice the fear that Allen might have been killed. Dixie Kirk sat by the revived camp fire, cursing under his breath over his failure to get Allen, and hoping that Allen had died.

His vengeful wish was denied when Allen came riding to the camp a few minutes later. A joyous shout went up when he appeared. Toothpick and Bad Bill rushed out to meet him. He looked exhausted.

"Gosh, Jim, I thought maybe something'd happened to you," Toothpick gasped in relief.

"Shucks, I ain't hurt none," Allen answered in a flat tone. "Better tell me how we come out, Toothpick."

"Why, the Yuma Kid got it, so did Frank Mills," Toothpick answered slowly. "Bad Bill was nicked, and I got a little scratch, and so did some of the others, but that's all. We got us eight prisoners."

"Do you know if Captain Painton was there?" Bad Bill Rodgers asked quickly.

"Yeah, he was there, but he got away," Allen answered.

"Got away? He slipped us?"

"Yeah. Which means that it's all a failure. We ain't any closer now to getting him than we ever was. It's just like we've got to start all over again," Allen explained slowly.

"Gosh, Jim, maybe now he'll dig in deeper so we can't ever find him," Toothpick suggested ruefully.

"I reckon he'll dig in deeper, all right," Allen answered. "But I'm goin' to find him, anyway. I ain't ever goin' to stop tryin' to get him. If I never do, then it'll be because I died first."

"Plenty of other skunks have tried to finish you, but you've got 'em, Jim," Toothpick encouraged.

"Yeah, but Captain Painton has got more brains than the others," Allen answered. "It looks like he outwitted me this time."

PAINTON STRIKES BACK

NEXT MORNING CARSON BUZZED WITH TALK OF THE fight between Allen's Outlaw Legion and the gang. Many wild stories circulated, some to the effect that the battle had cost Allen most of his men. These rumors were definitely discredited in mid-morning when the Outlaw Legion came riding into town like a triumphant army, bringing their prisoners.

As soon as the work of locking up the prisoners was finished, Toothpick Jarrick hurried to Allen with a report.

"We hit the gang hard, Jim," he declared excitedly. "Six of the dope runners are dead. We got Bigfoot Johns, and Red Morgan, and Three-finger Johnson, and some more I never seen afore. Pat Garrett says Slats Ryon was wounded bad, too, so that puts him out of the game. It's the hardest blow we ever struck at 'em."

"Yeah, but it was a failure all the same," Allen answered morosely. "Captain Painton got away."

"Gosh, Jim, you oughtn't to think of it that way," Toothpick argued. "You'll get another chance at him."

"Yeah, but he slipped me," Allen answered dejectedly.

Allen refused to be cheered by anything that Toothpick could say. But Doc Candee, huddling his wounded arm close to him, moved about grinning broadly. He broke up Toothpick's arguments by remarking:

"Captain Painton's gettin' away means we ain't through fightin' him, so maybe I'll get a chance at him myself next time. It sure made me mad to have to stay here while everybody else was havin' all the fun."

"Yeah, and we never got in on it, either, Jim," exclaimed Tiny Tim Murphy, who had left his post on the tower during the height of the excitement. "Bob Bolton and Kip Jerome and me can't figure why you never let us in on it."

"Shucks, I had to leave somebody in Carson so the gang wouldn't suspect we was movin' agin' 'em," Allen answered. "Anyway, you're all three regular Rangers, and this was a job for wolves."

"The next time we ain't goin' to be left out of it, though," Big Bob Bolton exclaimed.

Allen heard footsteps in the outer office and looked through the doorway. He saw Amos Stringer striding into the room beside Captain Harrison. Stringer looked angry, but Harrison seemed grimly pleased. As Allen rose to face them, Toothpick asked quickly:

"What's that you got stuck in your pocket, Jim? It looks like somebody's hat."

"Yeah, and I'm goin' after the gent that owns it as soon as it gets quiet outside," Allen answered in a low tone. "I picked it up outside of Nine Mile Camp last night after the fight."

"Is it Captain Painton's?" Doc Candee asked quickly.

"Nope, but it belongs to his right-hand man," Allen answered. Then he approached his visitors so he would not be obliged to explain further.

Stringer's face was an angry red as he confronted Allen.

"You're going too far, Allen," he declared hotly. "I'm not going to stand for any wholesale killing such as your Legion did last night."

"I thought you wanted me to clean out the gang," Allen answered gently.

"Certainly, that's what you're here for, but you've got to keep within the law, whatever you do."

113

"Well, we wolfed the gang and got plenty of 'em," Allen answered. "What are you aimin' to do about it?"

Stringer sputtered with wrath. "You've defied me. I won't stand idly by and see you do it again. It's hopeless. This State is turning into a nest of killers. I warned you this would happen, Harrison, when you put an outlaw in command of the Rangers down here."

"It's the only way," Harrison answered grimly.

Amos Stringer continued to express his displeasure at the turn events had taken. Knowing that Captain Painton had escaped, he stressed this fact in an attempt to show that Allen's methods were ineffective and should be changed.

Allen made no reply to this argument, but left the attorney general to Captain Harrison. He went into the front office and waited until he was sure that the excitement in the streets had quieted down, then he stepped outside.

One of the prominent buildings on River Street was that occupied by the Carson *Clarion*. From the first, the newspaper, edited by Ed Blendine, had bitterly denounced the Outlaw Legion, in an attempt to turn public opinion against Allen.

The little Ranger strode down the street to the door of the newspaper office and stepped inside. Near the front window, at a desk, was Ed Blendine, a massive, bald-headed man, with shining red cheeks and furtive eyes. When Allen entered he jerked up with surprise.

"What do you want in here?" he asked bluntly.

"You run a 'Lost and Found' column, don't you?" Allen asked quietly.

"Sure. Do you want to run an ad?" Blendine answered with a sneer.

"Yeah. I found a hat, and I reckon the owner of it might want it back," Allen answered.

As he spoke he removed the folded hat from the pocket of his tattered uniform coat, and held it toward Blendine. Blendine grew pale. But he quickly recovered from his confusion and prepared to write down Allen's ad.

"Maybe it would be a waste of time puttin' it in the paper, though," Allen remarked quietly. "There's two initials stamped in the band that'll help me find the owner. The initials are 'E. B.' "

"What're you drivin' at, Allen?" Blendine demanded gruffly.

"The initials are the same as yours. Maybe this is your hat," Allen remarked.

"I never saw it before," Blendine stated flatly.

"It's a gray hat, and I've seen you wearin' a gray hat a lot," Allen went on calmly. "You better try it on, Blendine. Maybe it'll fit you."

"It ain't my hat, and you know it, Allen."

Allen's face was hard as stone. "Anyway, it belongs to one of the gang that was in the fight last night," he declared. "It was lost in the confusion. It sort of brands the man who owns it as bein' one of the gang."

"I tell you it ain't mine," Blendine snapped.

"You can prove that by tryin' it on. If it don't fit you, then it's proof it ain't yours," Allen suggested shrewdly.

"I won't do anything of the sort," Blendine roared.

With a sudden movement he snatched the hat out of Allen's hand and flung it aside. Allen's eyes became flecked with yellow and he stared into the newspaper editor's eyes. He remarked gently:

"You're usin' your left hand this mornin', Blendine. I always thought you was right-handed. What's the matter with your right arm?"

As he spoke, Allen reached out quickly and gripped the man's right arm. Instantly a howl of pain came from Blendine. He cursed and drew back swiftly, tearing loose from Allen's grasp.

"Your right arm's hurt," Allen stated flatly. "Looks like maybe you was in a fight yourself and got nicked."

"Get out of here, Allen. You can't accuse me," Blendine cried.

"I am accusin' you," Allen remarked. "You were at Nine Mile Camp last night. You lost your hat in the fight and got wounded."

"Nothing of the sort. I lost that hat weeks ago out on the desert and the wind must've blown it near Nine Mile Camp. I hurt my arm workin' on the big press yesterday," Blendine gasped.

"Then you admit the hat is yours," Allen caught him up quickly. "Shucks, you're sure a plumb inexpert liar, Blendine."

"You dare call me that!"

Blendine reached awkwardly for the gun he wore under his coat. When his hand reached its butt, however, he realized the foolhardiness of the move. He quickly let go of the gun and blustered.

"Sure I'm callin' you a liar," Allen declared flatly. "Also, you're a killer and one of the leaders of the gang. You've been takin' over Laughin' Ed's job with Captain Painton since Laughin' Ed stretched rope. Now, unless you want to end up the same way he did, you better clear out of Carson and stay out."

"You orderin' me?" Blendine raged.

"That's exactly what I'm doin'. I could arrest you right now for bein' one of the gang, but I ain't goin' to waste any time gettin' rid of you. I'm givin' you till

116

sundown to clear out of Carson for good. If you ain't gone by dark I'll wolf you."

Allen deliberately turned his back and walked to the door. Again Blendine's hand moved toward his gun. He had an excellent opportunity for putting a bullet into Allen's back; but he did not even draw his weapon. He knew that Allen's death would bring the Legion down on him instantly, and the human wolves would tear him to pieces.

He sank into his chair, his forehead wrinkled with thought. His cunning mind was already beginning to evolve a plan for getting rid of Allen. His eyes glittered with the murderous hatred of a killer.

When the sun sank that day, Jim-twin Allen was standing in the door of the Ranger headquarters looking across the street at the front of the *Clarion* office.

Ed Blendine came out of the newspaper office and locked the door behind him, then swung into the saddle of his horse. He had a blanket roll tied behind the cantle, which contained some of his belongings. To all appearances he was obeying Allen's orders and preparing to leave Carson.

As he rode along River Street and passed the Ranger headquarters he did not glance left or right. He rode straight out of town. At the very edge of Carson he glanced back and saw that Allen was gone.

A grim, hard smile twisted Ed Blendine's merciless mouth. He dug in his spurs and traveled at a faster speed as darkness began to settle.

When he was miles away from Carson he shifted off the main road and took a short cut toward Steer Mountain. Blendine knew that one of Captain Painton's hide-outs was located on Steer Mountain and he was heading toward it.

After a few minutes of climbing, he was surprised to hear the noise of another horse ahead. Someone else was using the trail and had begun to climb it ahead of him.

He rode cautiously, listening all the while. He sensed that the other man had heard him and was taking precautions. Then the noises ceased completely. Blendine believed that the other rider had hidden on the side of the trail and was waiting for him to come along.

Blendine gripped his gun and made ready for an attack. He could not know whether the man ahead was friend or foe. It might be a member of the gang or a Ranger. Then Blendine heard a twig snap just ahead and pulled up short. He demanded suddenly:

"Who's there?"

There was silence for a moment, and then a voice answered: "If you're a Ranger, come ahead and get plugged."

"I'm not a Ranger," Blendine snapped. "Who are you?"

"A brother," the answer came.

"What's your name?"

"My password is tequila," the hidden man answered. "What's yours?"

"Durango."

Then in an easier tone the unseen man remarked: "Come ahead, then, Blendine. This is Dixie Kirk."

Reassured, Blendine prodded his horse upward on the trail. A movement came out of the darkness and Dixie Kirk rode into sight. When they were close together, the two men stopped and eyed each other to further reassure themselves.

"Why're you headin' this way, Kirk?" Blendine demanded.

"Captain Painton sent for me," Dixie Kirk answered shortly. "I sure ain't hankerin' to see him, but I reckon it's wiser for me to go than to stay away."

"Damn right it is," Blendine stated bluntly. "Ride ahead. I'll follow you."

Kirk complied. Blendine followed him closely as the trail curled and twisted up the mountainside. They spent an hour in laborious climbing, while neither of them spoke.

Then the two were immediately challenged by a sentry, armed with a rifle. Blendine identified himself and Kirk, and they moved on.

There was a cabin under some trees on the far side of a clearing, but it seemed to be absolutely dark and deserted. Blendine knew, however, that the windows were thickly covered with paper and blankets, so that not one stray gleam of light from inside could shine through. He and Kirk dismounted at the door of the cabin, and Blendine rapped.

"Come in," the cold voice of Captain Painton answered.

They pushed open the door and were met by a blinding glare of light reflected from a sheet of tin held behind the flame of a lamp. In the shadow on the other side of the room, Captain Painton stood, eying them while they could not see him. Then he tossed the reflector aside, and he appeared out of the blackness.

"I never ordered you to come here, Blendine," Captain Painton said harshly.

"No, but Jim Allen ordered me out of town," Blendine answered angrily. "I come here because I've got a plan for strikin' back at him."

Captain Painton stared at Blendine with his cold, sharklike eyes. Then with a gesture he declared:

"I'll talk to you later, Blendine. I sent for Kirk." He turned to Dixie Kirk, who was shifting from foot to foot uneasily, and growled: "You've failed, like every one else. You promised to get Allen, and you haven't done it. Are you yellow?"

Kirk stiffened. "You can't say that about me. I been tryin' to find a chance to shoot Allen, but the right time didn't come. I've sworn to get him. All I need is the chance."

"You had your chance last night. You were with Allen when he attacked my meeting at Nine Mile Camp. Why didn't you get him then?"

"Because he kept out of sight. I was itchin' to drill him, but I couldn't find him in the dark. He ain't human. He disappeared into thin air."

Captain Painton laughed mockingly. "He slipped you. I warned you what would happen to you if you failed to get him, Kirk."

"All I need is the chance," Kirk protested anxiously. "I ain't goin' to rest till I've filled him full of lead."

"Lucky for you you ain't dead already for your failure," Captain Painton exclaimed. "You not only didn't get Allen, but you failed to warn me about his plans. As a result he captured eight of my men, killed six more, and wounded another dozen. I've made men step aside for falling down on matters far less important than that, Kirk."

"I tried twice to slip away and warn you, but both times I was stopped," Kirk pleaded uneasily. "There wasn't nothin' I could do but try to get Allen. If he hadn't hopped out of sight like a flea, I'd have plugged him sure."

120

"If the gang wasn't weakened by Allen's attack, you'd be eating daisy roots by now, Kirk. As it is, I'm forced to let you have one more chance. But if you fail to get Allen again I'll kill you with my own hands and leave you for the buzzards."

"I'll get him," Kirk promised wildly.

"Then you can go. No, wait, and leave with Blendine." He turned to the newspaper editor coldly. "So Allen ordered you out of town, did he? And you went like a licked dog."

"Yes, but it's only part of a plan I have in mind," Blendine answered quickly. "If I'd stayed there, Allen would have killed me, or thrown me into the lockup. I left to make him think I was afraid of him. I've thought of a way of striking back."

"What is it?" Painton demanded.

"The whole Outlaw Legion is in Carson now," Blendine began to explain. "Allen's called them in from the camp on Mesa Verde. They're all over town, but mostly they hang around the Ranger headquarters. While they're there they won't be expectin' us to make any move against them, especially now. I figure that this is the time to strike."

"How?" Painton asked sharply.

"By gatherin' the gang together and attackin' them in town," Blendine answered. "We can take them by surprise, just as they took us last night. They won't be prepared for any such move on our part. We'll be down on them before they even know what's happening. We'll cut their strength in half and perhaps wipe out all of them, including Allen."

Captain Painton's gray eyes glared in contempt. "And I suppose you want to lead the attack, Blendine?" he asked bitterly.

121

"I'll do it. I'll be glad of the chance to fight the Legion when the advantage of surprise is on our side," Blendine answered grimly.

"The plan is a good one. In fact, I've been planning almost exactly the same thing since this morning," Captain Painton declared. "I've already issued orders for my men to gather together near Salt Fork tomorrow at high noon."

"Then we'll do it?" Ed Blendine exclaimed.

Captain Painton nodded. "Certainly. Allen and his men are probably expecting us to keep out of sight for a time, after last night. Furthermore, they will hardly expect us to hit back at them in broad daylight. That's why I've set the time for noon tomorrow."

Dixie Kirk spoke up quickly. "That'll give me the best possible chance to get Allen. He won't have any chance to keep out of sight. I'll get him when nobody else is lookin'."

Captain Painton nodded stiffly again. "That's why I'm lettin' you live a little longer, Kirk. Allen won't be expecting a bullet to come from one of his own men," he asserted grimly. "We'll have him between two fires. You and Blendine will both try to get him. Very likely the Legion will be caught in the street, and they'll have no chance of gettin' back into the headquarters building to protect themselves."

"That's true; they're usually all over the streets," Ed Blendine exclaimed. "As soon as I lead the gang into town, I'll start lookin' for Allen."

"You?" Captain Painton sneered. "You're not going to lead my men tomorrow, Blendine. I'm going to lead them myself."

"What? Come out in the open?" Blendine gasped. "That's a big chance to take. You've never done anything like that before."

"I've never done it before because it's never been necessary until now," Captain Painton declared. "I can no longer issue orders blindly. I've got to be on the spot to see that they're carried out to the letter. I am not going to take any chances that this new plan will fail. Allen is pressing me too hard."

"But Allen knows what you look like. If he sees you he'll go for you," Blendine protested. "He's faster with his guns than you—"

"True," Captain Painton nodded. "Allen is faster with his guns; but I don't intend that he should see me. I am going to keep out of sight and direct the movements of my men. I will leave Allen to you two. Tomorrow at high noon he must die."

"We'll see to that," Dixie Kirk exclaimed vehmently.

"One or the other of us will get him," Blendine agreed.

"Then that's all," Captain Painton stated flatly. "Be at Salt Fork tomorrow in plenty of time, and see that you have plenty of cartridges. Before we're through with Allen and his Legion, Carson will be the scene of a real massacre!"

HIGH NOON

BAD BILL ROGERS STRODE EXCITEDLY INTO THE Ranger headquarters late the next morning bursting with an unusual bit of news.

"Jim, the *Clarion* office is closed," he said breathlessly. "There's a notice on the door signed Ed Blendine sayin' he ain't coming back."

"That so?" Allen asked, grinning broadly.

"Why, you danged little devil, you know all about it,

then," Bad Bill exclaimed disgustedly. "Who told you?"

"Shucks, that notice has been up there since last evenin'," Allen answered. "And I knowed it was goin' up afore Blendine put it there."

"You did? Then why is he gone?" Bad Bill asked quickly.

"He's just movin' to other parts for his health," Allen answered.

Though Bad Bill plied him with further questions, Allen remained silent.

"There's no use tryin', Bill," Doc Candee remarked as he sat on the edge of his bunk. "That darn little half pint never talks at all, except when he's pryin' something loose from the back of your head that he wants to know."

Just then Captain Harry Harrison strode through the front door. He smiled broadly at Allen.

"You've got Amos Stringer worked up plenty, Allen," he remarked. "Don't you go worryin' about him none. He's just a cantankerous old cuss that can't help arguin' with folks."

"Sometimes I think he's more'n that," Allen answered cryptically.

"What do you mean?" Harrison asked.

"Why, I mean that it ain't always easy to understand people. Stringer gets mean sometimes, but at other times he's as gentle and kind as any man who ever lived. I seen him fussin' around Mrs. Stringer and helpin' her like she was everything in the world to him. Yes, sir, he's plumb different at times."

"That reminds me, Amos went over to Birchill this mornin' to see Marshal Hooker about a case, and Mrs. Stringer's comin' over here to see you in a few minutes, Jim," Captain Harrison said. "Jeff Gordon just brought her to town in the buggy. She's down the street now, waitin' while Jeff does some buyin' in the store. I stopped and spoke to her, and she said she wants to congratulate you on fightin' the gang like you did night before last."

"Shucks, she sure is a kind lady," Allen said softly. "I can't imagine how she can be so nice to a no-account gent like me."

"She don't think you're no account," Captain Harrison went on. "I reckon she and Nora think mighty high of you."

"It's because of people like them that I'm fightin' Captain Painton's gang," Jim Allen remarked softly. "They're so fine I'd do anything in the world for 'em."

Captain Harrison was about to comment when they were startled by the sound of a horse running down River Street at full speed. They looked up just in time to see it rear and stop near the hitch rack outside. Toothpick jumped out of the saddle and hastened to the door as fast as he could swing his long legs. His face was a picture of dismay and anxiety.

"Jim, the gang's ridin' into town!" he gasped.

Allen jerked to his feet. For a moment he was speechless, then he blurted:

"Where're they comin' from? How many of 'em? What do you think they're aimin' to do?"

"They're comin' from the west," Toothpick exclaimed. "There must be twenty or thirty of 'em, and they're all masked. Some of 'em are carrying rifles besides their six-guns. It looks like they're comin' to pay us back for what we did to 'em the other night."

"Who's leadin' 'em?" Allen asked quickly.

"Don't know. I just saw 'em comin' in the distance. They're goin' to be here pronto."

Captain Harrison immediately glanced at Allen. He hurried to the door, then stopped and listened. The others could hear nothing, but when Allen turned back it was as though he had verified Toothpick's assertion by means of the faint sounds his keen ears had caught. At the same time King growled and hurried to Allen's side, swinging his bushy tail. Allen ordered quickly:

"Get the Legion together quick. Tell 'em to line the streets. Tell everybody else to stay plumb out of sight."

With a whoop Toothpick went dashing out with Bad Bill Rogers after him. Doc Candee jerked up from his bunk and reached for his six-gun, which was hanging on a nail. Allen hurried through the doorway, ran to the middle of the street, and looked into the distance. He could see a cloud of dust stirred up by the riders rushing upon Carson.

"Come on, wolves!"

Toothpick's bellow was answered by a moment of silence. Then members of the Legion began pouring out of the doors along the street.

The three regular Rangers, Tiny Tim Murphy, Big Bob Bolton, and Kip Jerome, burst out of a restaurant across the way.

Behind them came Dixie Kirk. His eyes were gleaming with a sly grimness, and his thin lips were curled into an evil smile. He hurried toward Allen. Knowing that the time for the gang's attack had arrived, he wished to get as close to Allen as possible.

"Wait till they start firin'," Allen shouted. "Keep in the open all you can. Don't let up till they're all dead or drove out."

He whirled quickly and hurried back to the headquarters building. Dixie Kirk followed him grimly. Allen turned at the door, let Kirk pass him, then slammed it shut. Doc Candee was still in the office, grasping his six-gun.

"I'm goin' to get in on this fight," he declared tersely.

"All right, Doc, you guard this door," Allen commanded crisply. "Kirk, you stay by the windows. If any of the gang comes in, drop 'em in their tracks. They might try to get our prisoners loose."

Allen turned and started for the rear office. Candee asked him quickly:

"Where you goin', Jim?"

"After dope runners," Allen called over his shoulder. "Both of you stay here. I'll be back."

Suddenly the advancing gang swept down upon Carson like a tornado. As they rushed along the main street, guns began to bark. Shouts and whoops mixed with the echoing reports.

The riders fired rapidly, sending bullets toward every doorway, trying to pick off every man they glimpsed. Windows fell splintering to the streets. Horses squealed and whinnied. The attacking party was all masked. Above the handkerchiefs drawn across their faces, their evil eyes gleamed.

"Look at 'em, the skunks," Doc Candee exclaimed wrathfully.

He crouched at the edge of one of the windows, ready to fire if any of the gang should charge toward the building. Then he glanced aside and saw Dixie Kirk looking around.

"Pay attention to the street, Kirk," he ordered bluntly. "Your job's to keep those coyotes away from here."

Kirk obeyed, his face flushed an angry red. Candee eyed him suspiciously, then looked around for Allen. On a sudden notion he hurried into the small rear office. It was empty. Then he hurried back to his station.

"Allen's slipped out the back way," he gasped. "He's probably in the thick of the fight right now."

Dixie Kirk jerked around and stared. Suddenly he realized that again his plan was frustrated. He had intended to stay in the street, where he would have an opportunity of shooting Allen. Instead, he found himself shut up inside the office with Doc Candee, his chance gone. Wrathfully he hurried toward the rear office.

"Where you goin', Kirk?" Doc Candee snapped at him.

"After Allen. I'm worried about him," Kirk lied.

Doc Candee laughed shortly. "He can take care of hisself. He don't need help from you or anybody else. He ordered you to guard these windows and you better do it. You know I've got a bad arm and can't shoot straight."

Dixie Kirk cursed under his breath. He was forced to abandon his purpose and return to the windows. He realized that Candee was suspicious of him. For a moment he considered killing Candee on the spot, then going off on a search for Allen.

He realized quickly, however, that the act might prove his undoing, for after that he would be forced to fly. He remembered Captain Painton's threat and knew he must be extremely careful. Huddling by the window, he peered out in the hope that he might see Allen and find a chance to shoot.

When Allen slipped out of the rear door of the headquarters building, he ran along the narrow alley until he reached a space between two of the structures. He slipped into it and rapidly worked his way toward the street. There he paused, cuddling his twin Colts.

He stared in the direction from which the attacking

party was riding, into each masked face that came within sight. Grimly, and with a certain hopelessness, he hunted for the man known as Captain Painton.

When Allen turned and looked in the other direction, his blood ran cold. In front of the store was a two-seated buggy, and in the rear seat was Mrs. Stringer. She was staring with terrified eyes at the gang riders who were rushing toward her. The horses harnessed to the buggy were dancing with fright.

As Allen looked he saw Jeff Gordon come hurrying from the store, stop an instant on the sidewalk, then dash for the buggy.

The attack had come so swiftly that it had taken Jeff Gordon and Mrs. Stringer completely by surprise. Before Gordon had time to climb to the front seat of the buggy, four of the gang riders rushed past.

They fired wildly, aiming at Jeff Gordon. The blasting reports made the horses rear, then suddenly bolt forward. None of the bullets touched Gordon, but when the buggy dashed ahead, he was thrown backward. He stumbled and sprawled on the sidewalk, stunned. Mrs. Stringer grasped the back of the front seat rigidly as the buggy lurched and the horses dashed wildly down the street.

It happened in a few seconds. Mrs. Stringer tried to reach forward and grasp the reins, but her lameness hampered her, and she found them beyond her reach. The next instant, as the horses broke into a gallop, the reins went flying in the air. Allen had seen the whole thing. Mrs. Springer's plight drove even the attack of the gang from his mind. He leaped from the narrow space between the buildings and ran toward the buggy as it rushed by.

He could not reach it in time. The pair of horses

flashed past like black lightning. Unable to catch up with the buggy on foot, Allen could only watch them speed out of reach. He whirled, intending to rush to the space behind the headquarters building, where Princess was tethered, and give chase, but as he moved, a startling sight stopped him. One of the gang riders sped past the buggy, then whirled and began to race after it.

For an instant Allen glimpsed the eyes of the man attempting to stop the runaway horses. They were cold and gray. The handkerchief covering the man's face bulged out at his chin where it covered a thick beard.

When Allen realized that it was Captain Painton who was trying to save Mrs. Stringer, he was paralyzed with surprise. In an instant he recovered and jerked out his guns. Here was the man whom he had sworn to get, and this was his chance. But he realized that to shoot Captain Painton would be equivalent to killing Mrs. Springer.

Grimly Allen withheld his fire, unaware of the danger to which he was exposing himself by remaining in the open.

Within the space of a few seconds the buggy and Captain Painton were almost all the way through the town. Their rush had sent the masked riders swerving aside and for a moment there was a break in the fight; then it was quickly resumed. Allen's mind raced for a way out of his predicament. He realized that though he dared not stop Captain Painton now, he could give chase. He turned to dart to the rear of the buildings.

As Allen moved, a six-gun roared almost in his ear. He felt a burning pain in his side and knew he was hit. He gave a leap that carried him yards away, at the same time his twin Colts streaked out. When he struck the road again he was facing in the opposite direction. One

130

of the masked riders had drawn to a stop close to him and fired point-blank. Even as Allen's gun came out, another bullet sped on its way toward him.

Allen leaped and flame and smoke poured out of his guns. The reports were like a long roll of thunder. The masked man on the horse fired again, but Allen was an elusive target. The fusillade from Allen's guns struck him with such force that he was carried out of the saddle. He struck the road, rolled over twice, and lay still.

Allen whirled about, to make sure that none of the other masked riders was bearing down on him. Then he strode to the dead man with slow, deliberate movements. Stooping, he caught hold of the kerchief covering his assailant's face and jerked it down. When he straightened, Allen's face looked even older and more inhuman than before.

"I told you you'd get wolfed if you ever came back to Carson, Ed Blendine," he said coldly.

Ed Blendine stared at the sky with glazing eyes. He had learned that Allen always kept a promise.

The wound in Allen's side burned like fire. Setting his lips grimly against the pain, he started again for the narrow space between the buildings. He slid through, then ran awkwardly toward the rear of the headquarters building. He stumbled and tottered as the pain of his wound throbbed through his whole body, but he forced himself on.

When Allen reached the space where Princess and Honey Boy were tied, the battle broke out with fresh vigor.

Quickly he loosened Princess and pulled himself on her back. She realized that he was hurt, and whinnied a shrill protest. Allen forced her around the building to the street.

As he sped past the headquarters, he glanced at the windows and saw Dixie Kirk peering at him. Kirk made a quick movement to raise his gun, but the next instant Allen was out of sight behind the adjoining building. Allen left the fighting in the street to the others, and urged Princess in the direction which the runaway horses had taken.

Toothpick rode across his path, firing rapidly with two guns at a pair of fleeing gang riders. Allen called to him swiftly:

"Follow me, Toothpick!"

Toothpick heard the call and detected the anguish in Allen's voice. He was loath to leave the fight, but he sensed that Allen needed him. He saw his captain roll sightly in the saddle, then glimpsed the red splotch on the side of Allen's ragged coat.

"He's been hurt," Toothpick gasped.

A masked rider rushed for Allen, but Toothpick sent a bullet whizzing through the man's hat and stopped the attack. Grimly Toothpick swung around, intending to keep the others away from Allen at any cost. But no one was following now. Toothpick raced ahead, eying Allen worriedly, half expecting him to tumble out of the saddle at every bound Princess made. But Allen clung tightly, his shoulders hunched and legs dangling.

Less than two miles outside of town Allen saw the buggy drawn to a stop at the side of the road. Mrs. Stringer was still sitting in the rear seat, and now she was clinging desperately to the reins as the horses tossed their heads wickedly.

Toothpick gave an exclamation of dismay when he realized what had happened. Allen's hands were on his guns, but Captain Painton was not in sight.

Disappointment of the keenest sort filled him when he saw that Painton was gone.

He dropped out of the saddle and tottered toward the buggy. Mrs. Stringer gave a little cry when she saw that Allen was wounded.

"You all right?" Allen asked quickly.

"Yes, Yes," Mrs. Stringer gasped. "But you're hurt, Jim Allen. You shouldn't have followed me."

"Shucks, it was nothin'," Allen sighed. "Where's the gent that stopped the wild hosses for you? Where'd he go?"

"I hardly know, I was so stunned," Mrs. Stringer answered quickly. "He gave me the reins and rode away before I could even thank him."

"Do you know who he was? Did you recognize him?" Allen demanded swiftly.

"I hardly saw his face. His back was turned all the while he was in the buggy. Then he pulled his hat down when he gave me the reins and got back on his horse. I couldn't get a good look at him. But even if he's one of the dope runners, I owe him my life."

"I reckon you do, ma'am," Allen said grimly.

Toothpick noticed that an expression of great relief came over Allen's face when Mrs. Stringer asserted that she had not recognized the man who had saved her. A deep sigh came from Allen's lungs and he asked:

"Which way did he go?"

"South," Mrs. Stringer answered. "Jim Allen, you mustn't think of following him. You're hurt, and you need a doctor's attention."

"Nope," Allen countered, wagging his head stubbornly. "I can see a doctor later. I'm goin' to follow that gent—nothin' can stop me."

133

"But you can't," Mrs. Stringer cried. "You can't ride when you're hurt so badly."

"That's right, Jim, you're hard hit," Toothpick exclaimed anxiously. "You get into the buggy, and I'll take you back to Carson."

"Nope," Allen refused again. "I brung you along so you could take Mrs. Stringer back. Keep her safe. I've got a trail to follow and no time to waste."

Before they could stop him, he slipped onto Princess's back and started away. He rode quickly, searching the ground for sign, not realizing that he was leaving a trail behind him—a trail of bright-red drops on the grass.

A SECRET MISSION

FOR A SHORT TIME AFTER ALLEN RACED AWAY IN pursuit of Captain Painton, chaos filled Carson. Then the gang riders realized that they had no leader and became demoralized. Captain Painton had disappeared; Ed Blendine was lying dead in the road; no one was left in command. The fearful confusion ended when the masked gang began to rush out of town.

The Outlaw Legion, led by Bad Bill, immediately gave chase. For a while the two groups of riders exchanged shots as they flew along the road. Then the Legion began to run out of ammunition and they were forced to abandon the fight. At the same time the gang scattered, so the chase became impossible.

The returning Rangers found the streets filled with men and women and frightened children. Excitement was running high, for it was plain to be seen that the gang had suffered serious losses. Twelve of them had been killed and many others wounded, while not one of the Outlaw Legion had been lost.

Hasty Hugh Higgins's arm had been broken by a bullet, George Cole was nursing an injured leg, and Pat Garrett had suffered another wound, but otherwise there were no casualties. When it was discovered how decisively the Legion gang had defeated the gang, a triumphant shout went up.

Toothpick Jarrick came driving along River Street, handling the reins of the buggy. Jeff Gordon saw the vehicle coming and rushed forward. When he saw that Mrs. Stringer was unhurt, his relief was so overwhelming that he broke down and cried like a baby. Toothpick left them together, then hastened to join the group of Rangers.

"Where's Jim?" Captain Harrison bellowed at the top of his voice.

"He's ridin' trail," Toothpick explained. "He shouldn't be doin' it either, 'cause he's hurt, but I couldn't stop him."

"Maybe we better go chase him and bring him back," Harrison suggested anxiously.

"Shucks, wild hosses couldn't drag Jim back now," Toothpick asserted. "There ain't nothin' to do but let him go."

Dixie Kirk was baffled and silent. Again Jim twin Allen had escaped him, and he was in a bitter humor, although he was forced to make himself appear jubilant.

All during the fight he had been obliged to remain inside the headquarters building with Doc Candee, and he had not been able to fire a shot. Remembering Captain Painton's threat that he must die if Allen did not, he grimly promised himself that Allen would not elude him a third time.

While the Legion celebrated their victory by swarming into the bars, Toothpick Jarrick, Doc Candee, and Captain Harrison returned to the headquarters building. Toothpick laughed uproariously as he began to clean his gun.

"Gosh, they come sweepin' down on us like they was goin' to wipe us off the face of the earth; instead they near got wiped out theirselves," he exclaimed. "Jim, sure didn't waste any time gettin' us organized agin' 'em."

"Jim Allen's the best Ranger we ever had, even if he is an outlaw," Captain Harrison declared sincerely. "Wait till Amos Stringer hears about this; he'll be hoppin' mad."

"Yeah, because this time he can't lecture us, we only defended ourselves," Doc Candee exclaimed, and they all laughed.

"You got any idea who Allen is trailin', Toothpick?" Captain Harrison asked.

"I can't figger it out at all," Toothpick answered worriedly. "First that buggy went runnin' out of town with Mrs. Stringer in it, and one of the gang riders chasin' it. Whoever he was, he forgot all about the fightin' and thought of nothin' but savin' Mrs. Stringer. Then Jim went slopin' after him, but by the time we reached the buggy the masked man was gone. There's only one gent that Jim's dead set on gettin', and that's Captain Painton."

"You mean that the man who stopped the runaways was Captain Painton?" Harrison asked quickly.

"He might have been, and that makes it all the harder to figure out," Toothpick answered, frowning. "I saw Jim's face when Mrs. Stringer said she never recognized that gent, and he sure looked relieved to hear it."

"You think he knows who Captain Painton really is?" Harrison demanded breathlessly.

"He might," Toothpick asserted. "I bet that if we only knew what was goin' on inside of Jim Allen's head right now, we'd be plumb surprised."

"I reckon we would," Captain Harrison agreed. "I hope he comes right back to Carson."

But that hope was in vain.

At sunset Allen rode slowly across Ash Meadows, miles from Carson. He drooped in the saddle, pressing one hand to the wound in his side. The loss of blood had weakened him, and the pain had grown more intense. At times his head sank forward, he gripped the pommel to keep himself from falling to the ground. Princess tossed her head protestingly. Yet Allen kept pressing on grimly.

Captain Painton had disappeared completely. During the first few hours of the chase, Allen had been able to follow his trail, but soon even that had vanished. Hunt as closely as he might, he had not been able to find any sign to follow once he lost the trail. In the hope of picking it up again, he had covered most of the territory south of Carson, but without success.

Usually Allen's keen senses enabled him to follow marks which other men could not see at all, but the pain of his wound numbed him. Sometimes he could see only a blur as the ground moved beneath Princess's hoofs. Sheer grit forced him on.

For a while he rode with legs dangling and head drooping forward; then he pulled himself up and looked around. He drew firmly on Princess's reins and muttered:

"Gosh, old lady, you stop that. You're headin' back

137

to Carson and tryin' to get me to quit, but I ain't goin' to let you fool me. You keep headin' south."

Princess squealed her protest, but Allen forced her on.

He slowly crossed Ash Meadows and began to climb into the hills. The trail was narrow and difficult to follow, and there was only the dim light of the moon to show him the way.

An hour passed while he roamed over the hillside trails, though it seemed like an eternity to him.

"Hold on a minute, you old pie-eater," Allen whispered. "Looks like some marks here. I've got to look at 'em."

With the utmost care Allen slipped out of the saddle and lowered himself to the ground. For a moment he clung to Princess, steadying himself. With a valiant effort he forced his brain to clear, then turned away and began to inspect the ground closely.

His eyes seemed to trick him, and when a wave of dizziness passed through him, he lowered himself to his knees and crawled on.

The marks he saw might have told him a great deal, had he been in full command of his senses, but now they bewildered him. He could not tell whether he was actually seeing footprints, or whether they were imaginary. He supported himself on a rock, dragged himself up, and tottered forward again. Then suddenly he heard a loud, sharp click, felt his foot gripped as though by a powerful claw, and fell forward.

Princess squealed with fear as Allen tumbled. He lay still a moment, then hoisted himself on his elbows and tried to drag himself on. Something held him back. He rolled over and sat up, trying to see the thing that had caught his foot. New pain surged through him, so intense that he twisted his face with the agony. Then he

138

managed to see what had happened. He had stepped into a large trap, and it had closed on his heel.

He was so weakened that he could do nothing to release himself. Try as he might, he could not open the trap a fraction of an inch. Its grip on his heel was especially cruel because Allen was wearing soft moccasins. Had he been wearing boots, the stiff leather would have protected him, and he might have been able to slip out of the trap almost unharmed.

He tried to pull himself free, after loosening his high-topped moccasin, but even this attempt was futile. After a long struggle he toppled over, unconscious.

Princess saw him fall and tossed her head wickedly. She backed away and stood on the trail, mincing about nervously. Then she whirled suddenly and clattered down the slope. She galloped along the trail wildly, then when she reached level ground, raced away like the wind.

When the sun rose, consciousness slowly came back to Allen. He was too weak to make another attempt to free himself. The sun mounted higher and threw its blistering heat down on him as he mumbled incoherently. Then he grew quiet and listened to sounds that seemed to come from far away.

There was a noise on the trail. Someone was riding up the hillside. Princess was leading the way, while behind her rode a girl on a calico pony.

Nora Stringer looked fresh and lovely in the morning sunlight, but her eyes were worried. She watched Princess closely, and a glad cry came from her lips when the old gray suddenly turned off the trail, plunged through the bushes, then stopped and whinnied.

She jumped out of the saddle and hurried ahead.

139

When she saw Allen lying on the ground, his foot caught in the trap, she stopped in dismay.

She called Allen's name, but his only answer was a roll of his head. Realizing that there was no time to be lost, she immediately tried to release him from the trap. She grew pale as she realized how greatly he had suffered. She was forced to use all her strength, and she was almost exhausted herself, when at last she managed to open the trap and release Allen.

Then she looked around hurriedly. Hearing a faint splashing of water, she hunted its source.

In a few minutes she found a trickle of water flowing down the rocks from a small spring. She soaked her kerchief, gathered some of the water in her felt hat, and hurried back to Allen.

She bathed his hot forehead, and forced a few drops between his swollen lips. They helped revive him, for he opened his eyes and stared keenly into her face. He tried to speak, but his words were an unintelligible whisper.

Nora Stringer realized that Allen's condition was serious, and that he must have a doctor's attentions as soon as possible. Another girl might have lost her head, but she set about getting Allen onto Princess's back without regard to the difficulties involved. She lifted Allen almost bodily, and supported him upright. Then she helped him hop toward the trail. Princess stood quietly while she placed Allen's uninjured foot in the stirrup and helped him up.

Allen called upon his last strength to get into the saddle. Once on Princess's back, he sagged forward and clasped his arms around the old gray's neck. The girl quickly mounted her own pony, then turned down the trail, leading Princess.

Nora headed toward the Circle G Ranch. It was closer than Carson, and Allen's strength would be saved by taking him there. She rode as fast as she dared, while Princess glided along behind her.

After a long hour, they reached the gate of the Circle G and turned to the ranch house. They were nearing the porch when Jeff Gordon came outside. He gave a shout of dismay and rushed toward Allen.

Gorden carried Allen into the house, then immediately dispatched one of his cow-punchers for the doctor. Allen was put on a bed in one of the downstairs rooms, and Mrs. Stringer came in. She took charge and called for hot water and bandages. Sitting in a chair beside the bed, she hastily began to dress his wounds. Jeff Gordon poured a little whisky down Allen's throat, and it served to revive him.

"Shucks, I'm sure obliged to you," he said in a weak whisper.

"Jim Allen, you save your strength and don't talk," Mrs. Stringer told him firmly. "I'm going to take care of you, no matter what anybody says."

A faint smile formed on Allen's lips, and he made no further protest. Mrs. Stringer's gentle, soft touch was like a caress. He submitted to her ministrations gratefully.

Jeff Gordon drew Nora Stringer aside and asked anxiously: "How did you find him? How did he get into such a fix?"

"Why, I was riding Piebald across Ash Meadows, and I saw Allen's horse running along with her saddle empty. When Princess saw me, she turned and came toward me as though she wanted help. I let her lead me up into the hills, and that's how I found him."

"I heard he got wounded durin' the fight in Carson

141

yesterday, but went off trailin' somebody anyway," Jeff Gordon exclaimed. "He sure is a very nervy little cuss. I couldn't stand what he's been through already."

"He's got more nerve than anybody else I ever saw," Nora exclaimed.

"Yeah, and it's too bad he's hurt. That means he won't be able to keep up the fight on the dope-runnin' gang for a time."

When Doctor Bliss arrived from Carson, he was surprised to find Allen so well cared for. Mrs. Stringer had already done almost as much for him as the doctor would have done.

Bliss made sure that the wounds were clean, gave his patient a stimulant, and left orders that he must remain perfectly quiet.

As soon as the news of Allen's injury reached Carson, the whole Outlaw Legion rode to the Circle G in a body. Toothpick, Doc Candee, and Bad Bill, were insistent upon seeing Allen at once, but Mrs. Stringer firmly refused to allow it. They had brought King with them. The big wolf dog went to the door and moaned so pathetically that Mrs. Stringer let him in.

King immediately went to Allen, put his great forefeet on the edge of the bed, and peered at his master. Allen raised one hand weakly and ruffled his shaggy collar. King settled down beside the bed, as though to guard him, while Mrs. Stringer continued to refuse admission to the Outlaw Rangers.

Allen gained strength rapidly under Mrs. Stringer's care. One day the Legion came trooping in and surrounded the bed, and Allen joked with them, saying that he would be up in a few days and rejoin them. Mrs. Stringer answered this remark by stating that he was going to stay where he was until he had fully recovered from his experience.

"Shucks, I don't know what would have happened to me if it hadn't been for you, ma'am," Allen told her gratefully. "You've sure took wonderful care of me. And I reckon I owe my life to Nora, too. I wouldn't 've lasted much longer if she hadn't found me when she did."

"Why, Jim Allen, you know it was Princess that saved you," Nora told him with a smile.

"Nope, it was mostly you," Allen insisted. "I won't ever forget what you done for me, either. It's worth gettin' sick just to have your mother take care of me like she's done."

"It's an honor," Mrs. Stringer declared sincerely. "Now, don't you say anything more about it."

THE WHITE WOLF'S SECRET

ONE DAY, ABOUT TWO WEEKS AFTER ALLEN HAD BEEN brought to the Circle G, Mrs. Stringer, Jeff Gordon, and Nora were sitting on the porch talking. The subject of their conversation was Jim-twin Allen. Every day Mrs. Stringer found something new and interesting to say about Allen, and never tired of talking of him.

"He's a poor, lonely boy," she remarked sympathetically. "It's a pity that a man who wanders through life bringing happiness to others should have so little of it for himself."

"I reckon that's right," Jeff Gordon agreed.

Just then Mrs. Stringer looked up and saw Frank Wright, one of the Circle G punchers, coming toward the house leading Princess. She asked, quickly:

"Frank, why are you bringing Jim Allen's horse here, all saddled?"

"Why, he called me in a little while ago and asked me to get her ready," Wright answered.

"Now I wonder what he thinks he's going to do?" Mrs. Stringer asked anxiously. "He's in no condition to get up, let alone think of riding anywhere. Jeff, you go in and see—"

She broke off in dismay, for at that moment Allen appeared in the doorway, fully dressed. He was pale, and moved slowly, but his freckled face was split by a broad, loose grin. As he stepped forward he limped slightly. King came outside with Allen, wagging his bushy tail happily.

"Jim Allen, you go right back to bed," Mrs. Stringer commanded sternly.

"Shucks, I'm feelin' pretty good now, and I've got some business to attend to," Allen answered sheepishly.

"You're not nearly well enough to get up," Mrs. Stringer protested. "You've got to go back. Jeff, you stop him and make him behave."

Allen stepped off the porch and turned his strange, slanted eyes on Jeff Gordon. "I reckon you could do it if you wanted to," he remarked softly. "You could pick me right up and put me back in bed, but I'd get up again as soon as your back was turned. If you don't let me go now, I'll sneak off durin' the night when nobody's watchin'."

"Jim Allen!" Mrs. Stringer cried pleadingly.

"Gosh, I ain't aimin' to be ungrateful to you," Allen said sincerely. "I owe you and Nora everything in the world, and I'll never forget it. Only, I can't stay here any longer; I've got to be movin'. My job ain't finished yet, and there ain't any time to waste."

144

"No use tryin' to keep him from it, then," Jeff Gordon remarked to his sister. "Once he's made up his mind, nothin' can stop him."

"Then come back as soon as you can," Mrs. Stringer begged. "You must come back and stay until you're entirely well. I'll worry about you until I see you again."

Allen wagged his head slowly and pulled himself painfully onto Princess's back.

"I won't be showin' up again till my job's done," he said wistfully.

Then, urging Princess on, he trotted down the ranch road. Her eyes warmly sympathetic and full of admiration, Mrs. Springer watched him ride away with King pacing alongside.

As Allen traveled over the road to Carson, he watched the ground carefully. Now and then he slowed down and leaned over to inspect more closely the marks he was following. Twice he slipped out of the saddle and knelt in the dust, studying them. Each time he had a painful struggle getting back on Princess, but no murmur of complaint came from him. Then, halfway between the town and the Circle G, he stopped and looked off into the distance.

"Reckon he cut off the road here, old lady," he remarked softly. "His trail's clear, and I won't have any trouble followin' it later. We'll be comin' back soon."

Late in the afternoon he rode down River Street and stopped in front of the Ranger headquarters where his appearance created a sensation.

Toothpick, Doc Candee, and Bad Bill Rogers rushed out to meet him. They wrung his hand and slapped his back. Captain Harrison hurried out to join in with his greeting. Allen answered their solicitous questions by declaring that he was completely recovered.

"Come right on in, Jim," Captain Harrison urged. "The governor just arrived a little while ago. He was goin' out to the ranch to see you, but now you're here he won't have to."

"You've got the gang running now, Jim," Bill declared. "You're fighting them to a standstill. I guess this is answer enough to the folks who objected to you being made a Ranger."

"Yeah, but maybe they was right after all," Allen said slowly.

"What do you mean?" Governor Harrison boomed. "Why, you've done more to establish law and order down here than any other man could have ever done."

"Maybe so, but I reckon I've gone as far as I can," Allen answered. "I'm licked."

"Licked? Ho-ho-ho!" The governor's laughter shook the walls. "You've almost cleaned out the gang, then you say a thing like that. You mean Painton is licked."

"Nope," Allen answered solemnly, wagging his head. "I'm the one that's beat. I reckon there ain't nothin' left for me to do but resign from the Rangers and quit."

"Quit?" the men in the room chorused in dismay.

"Yeah, step out," Allen went on. "I reckon I belong on the long trail and not with the Rangers."

For a moment they were too appalled to speak. They stared at him as though they could not believe their ears. Yet there was no doubt that Allen was perfectly serious. The only man in the room who took heart at the announcement was Dixie Kirk, who was standing aside and eying Allen contemptuously.

"Jim, you can't mean that," Captain Harrison

exclaimed suddenly. "Why, you never did anything like this afore."

"Nope, I never did," Allen agreed sadly. "But I never been in such a fix afore. The only thing for me to do is back out."

They all began to talk at once, but Allen seemed scarcely to hear any of them. He sank into a chair looking more helpless than any one had ever seen before. He found it difficult to look into the faces of the men before him, for he saw reproach in their eyes.

"Jim, I don't believe for a minute you're backin' out on us," Captain Harrison declared stanchly. "What reason could you have for doin' such a thing?"

"I've got a powerful good reason," Allen said.

"What is it? We're entitled to know that, aren't we?"

"I reckon you are, but I can't tell you," Allen answered. "It ain't fair to you not to tell, but this time I've got to be unfair. If I told you it would hurt somebody else bad—somebody I would rather die than hurt."

"You mean you've found out who Captain Painton is?" Captain Harrison demanded shrewdly.

Allen hesitated before answering, then he nodded slowly. "Yeah, I know now who Captain Painton is. But I ain't never goin' to tell a soul."

They were silent and mystified. They looked at each other strangely. Governor Harrison seemed about to demand of Allen that he disclose the identity of Captain Painton, but his Ranger brother quickly gripped his arm and silenced him.

"Jim," Captain Harrison declared, "the only man who stands a chance of ever bringing the gang to justice is you. If we don't stamp them out now, they will rise to greater power than they had in the first place. We've got

147

them on the run, and if we don't finish the job, this State won't be a fit place to live in."

"And that ain't all," Toothpick said quickly. "You remember that Silver Conklin was killed durin' the first fight we ever had with the gang, and Silver was one of the finest gents that ever lived. You remember how we buried him, and promised him that we would never stop fightin' the gang till it was wiped out. Then there are the others: Pete Borden, and the Yuma Kid, and Frank Mills, and Lieutenant O'Brien, and Kansas Jones, and Dude Malone. They all died fightin' the gang, leavin' us to keep on fightin' 'em.

"Now, you've done so much already, Jim, and none of us could complain if you stepped out of the Rangers. Breakin' your promise to livin' men is one thing, but you couldn't break your promise to the men who died fightin' for you."

"No, I could never do that."

"Then you'll stick with us, Jim, and fight it out to the end?" Captain Harrison asked eagerly.

"I reckon that's what I've got to do," Allen answered slowly.

They whooped with joy and crowded around him. Their exuberance seemed to have no effect on him. He remained as morose as before. At last he backed away from them, and sidled toward the door.

"Where you goin', Jim?" Toothpick inquired anxiously. "We've sure missed you, and we wish you would stay here with us."

Allen smiled sadly. "I've been longin' to be with you again, too, but I reckon it ain't to be. I've got to go off by myself for a while and think things out."

They tried to detain him and cheer him up, but nothing they could say had any effect. He finally tore

148

away and slipped out the rear door. He quickly mounted Princess, rode to River Street, then started out of town. It was growing dark as he jogged along the road, with King following him.

In the Ranger headquarters, the men talked excitedly about Allen. During the conversation they did not notice that Dixie Kirk rose quietly, went into the back office, and did not return. Kirk quietly left the building, hurried around to the hitch rack, and mounted his horse. Then he started riding in the direction Allen had taken, his eyes shining with the grim brutality of a killer.

Allen made a decision as he rode through the darkness, along the road which connected Carson with the Circle G. His face remained hard and inhuman as though he had set himself a grim task. King trotted alongside Princess, looking again and again into Allen's face. They went on for miles, until they reached the spot where Allen had stopped on the way to Carson. There he paused, got down, and inspected the ground.

He saw a clear-cut trail and began to follow it. It lead southward, toward the Sangre de Dios Mountains and the Rio Grande.

It was past midnight when he reached the bank of the Rio. The river was smooth and tranquil, a broad silver band. Allen turned, following the trail along its course, toward the mountains. Soon he came to a thick woods which grew to the edge of the water. He entered the deep shadows slowly, looking ahead warily and listening. He was in the deepest part of it when Princess tossed her head and quickened her pace. Allen steadied her.

"You're smellin' another hoss, old lady," he said in a whisper. "There must be one hid somewheres around here close."

A few yards farther on he pulled to a stop and slipped out of the saddle. He skirted along the edge of the trail a short way, then came back and shifted to the other side.

Looking up, he saw a rude structure ahead, hidden under thick foliage. He crept toward it silently and saw that it was a ramshackle shed. Drifting toward the door he looked inside and saw that there was a horse in the stall.

Then he turned and stole back to Princess and pulled into the saddle.

"Yep, we found it," he said softly. "That means we're close. What we've found is only a hoss-changin' place, but I reckon there's a hide-out somewheres near."

He continued along cautiously. Princess moved soundlessly, winding her way through the trees. The trail almost disappeared, but to Allen's keen eyes there were signs that led him farther. Then he pulled Princess to a stop again. For a long time he sat in the saddle, listening. As last he slipped down and stooped to speak to King.

"Listen, old fellow," Allen whispered. "Go back along the trail and wait for me. Keep out of sight, and don't make a sound. Stay there till I come for you."

King whimpered, turned, and started away. He understood the directions with an almost human intelligence.

Allen watched him disappear in the blackness, then turned. The almost invisible trail led down the wooded slope. Through the trees he could see the Rio flowing past. Then he saw a log cabin in the shadows, almost at the edge of the water.

It was an ideal place for a hideaway. It was securely hidden; yet, even in case of a surprise, its occupant could slip quickly across the shallow river into Mexico and elude capture.

Grimly satisfied, Allen crept closer. The cabin was perfectly dark, but a horse was standing beneath the trees a few yards away, and that told Allen someone was inside. He moved toward the door so quietly that the horse gave no alarm.

For a long minute he stood by the door, listening. From inside came the sounds of movements. Allen's hands dropped to his twin Colts, then came up again and touched the door. Suddenly he stepped forward and, thrusting the door open, stepped inside the room.

Captain Painton was sitting at a rude table. Allen's entrance so startled him that he leaped back, overturning his chair. His hand flashed toward the gun strapped around his waist, but before he could touch it Allen said sharply:

"If you draw it, I'll kill you, but I ain't aimin' to kill you now."

Captain Painton froze. The ring in Allen's voice was more than enough warning. He moved his hand slowly away from his gun, and his eyes glittered coldly.

"That's better," Allen remarked.

Captain Painton was too dumfounded to speak for a moment. He lifted his hand, stroked his false beard, and slowly smiled.

"You've committed suicide by coming here tonight, Allen. The place is surrounded by my men, and you'll never get out alive."

"Nope, there ain't nobody here tonight but you," Allen answered promptly.

Captain Painton's eyes grew hard. Allen had stated the truth with an uncanny accuracy. Usually Painton surrounded himself by men paid to protect him, but tonight none of the gang was near.

151

"How did you find me, and what do you want?"

"I trailed you," Allen answered. "And I'm here to make a bargain with you."

"What kind of a bargain do you think can be made between you and me, Allen?"

"An understandin' that we've got to have. It's the only way you can go on livin'—by agreein' with me. I made up my mind to that since I found out who you are."

"You know who I am?" Captain Painton blurted, his voice trembling with dismay.

"I reckon I do. It ain't a guess, I'm sure of it. I've got all the proof I need," Allen answered grimly.

"I'm glad I've found it out and yet I'm sorry. Maybe it would've been better if I never found it out till after I killed you; but I'm glad I learned. I swore to kill you on sight, afore I knowed who you was, but now I don't want to do it. It's the first time I ever went back on my word."

Captain Painton blustered. "If you know so much, who am I?"

Allen's eyes gleamed. "You ain't one man; you're two. Half of you, the part that you've named Captain Painton, is cold-blooded and mean, and hates every human bein'. The other half is warm and kind. The reason I ain't puttin' a bullet into you now is because I can't kill the bad side without killin' the good—and I want the good to go on livin'."

Captain Painton stared at him.

"Then you do know!" he exclaimed. "Well, why don't you kill me? If you hate me so much, get out your guns right now. I admit I hate people; I hate them like poison, good and bad alike!"

"I understand why you feel like that, and so I can't

152

blame you," Allen answered slowly. "Only I know you're wrong about it. Somethin' happened to you that's preyed on your mind and warped it so you can't think straight any more."

Captain Painton gazed at Allen as though hypnotized. Allen went on calmly:

"You and me are a lot alike. You've got two sides to you, and so have I. One part of you is an upright citizen, and the other part is the devil hisself. One part of me is a man and the other part is a wolf. We're a devil and a wolf talkin' right now. Bein' like that, I can understand you better than anybody, and that's why I come here tonight to make a bargain."

"What is it?" Captain Painton demanded hoarsely.

"You've got to quit lettin' the devil part of you rule you. You've got to quit runnin' dope and disband the gang. Then you've got to forget that you ever was Captain Painton. Captain Painton has got to die, but I ain't goin' to kill him if I can help it—you are. You've got to wipe him off the face of the earth. If you do that, I won't harm you, but if you don't, then I'll live up to my oath and kill you myself."

"Why should I trust you?" Captain Painton gasped. "How do I know you won't go back on your word and expose me?"

"I'll never do that," Allen answered with grim sincerity. "If I did, it would kill the ones dear to you. I give you my word right here and now that nobody will ever find out from me your identity. If folks ever learn of it, it'll be because you brought it on yourself."

"That would never happen without your help. Nobody would ever find out about me unless you told them."

Allen remained silent a moment studying the face of the man on the other side of the table.

"I ain't expectin' you to give me an answer," Allen went on. "I don't need one from you. I'm tellin' you what you've got to do. Wipe Captain Painton out of the world so that he's never heard from again. Disband the gang and forget that it ever existed. Then no harm will ever come to you. But if you go on runnin' dope, if you go on bein' Captain Painton, then I swear I'll kill you."

"And expose me after death," Captain Painton cried.

"No, not even then. But I'll kill you," Allen declared flatly.

Then he turned and slipped out of the door. The move was so fast that he seemed to vanish from the cabin as if by magic. He ran across the open space beside the cabin and started to hurry up the slope toward the trail.

Suddenly the roar of a gun broke the stillness. A flash of flame came from the darkness near Allen. He stopped short in his tracks, then dropped to his knees. With a moan he rolled over. The ground was steep, and his lax body continued to tumble down the slope. Then it spilled off the edge of the bank, and he fell into the water of the river.

Dixie Kirk stared through the darkness, crouching behind the tree from which he had fired. His hard face was grimly set as he watched Allen roll down the slope into the river. Then he hurried forward, stopped at the edge of the bank, and peered downward. The sluggish water was quiet; there was no sign of Allen except his hat, which was floating slowly downstream.

Dixie Kirk grinned evilly, and he thrust his smoking gun into his holster.

"Allen's dead *now*," he declared hoarsely.

CALL TO THE WOLF PACK

WHEN ALLEN FAILED TO RETURN TO CARSON NEXT morning, grave concern was felt for him. Toothpick, Doc Candee, Bad Bill Rogers, and Captain Harrison talked worriedly, wondering if something had happened to him.

At any other time they would have accepted, Allen's absence without question, but they knew he was still weak and could not ride far, and they had expected him back before dark.

At the end of the first twenty-four hours of Allen's absence, Toothpick declared that he was going out and search. Doc Candee eagerly offered to go with him. They organized a search. Bad Bill and Captain Harrison were to ride east, while Toothpick and Doc went west. In this way they could cover the country thoroughly and rapidly.

They rode out of Carson quickly. Toothpick and Doc Candee began to scour Ash Meadows and the Sangre de Dios Mountains as best they could, while Bad Bill and Captain Harrison searched Mesa Verde and the Marching Men Hills. Each pair of men rode hard throughout the day and covered as much ground as possible. When sunset came, they had found no trace of Allen.

Worn and more worried than ever, they turned back to Carson. When they reached the town they saw the others riding in, looking solemn and exhausted. They did not need to speak a word with each other to know that the search had proved fruitless. They spent an extremely uneasy night and stayed awake in the hope that Allen would return at any time.

"He's been gone more'n two days now, and I know he never intended to stay so long because he didn't take any grub," Toothpick declared. "There's only one thing that makes me think Jim might be all right, and that's King. King went with him. If he'd met with an accident, King would sure enough be back here by now."

"Not if somethin' happened to King, too," Candee reminded the others.

"Yeah, that's right," Toothpick grumbled. "The whole durn gang might've been looking for Jim, and killed 'em both."

Doc Candee said suddenly: "And another thing, the new man, Dixie Kirk, ain't showed up since Jim left. I never trusted that gent. If anything happened to Jim, Kirk's behind it."

"Yeah, it sure looks bad," Captain Harrison remarked slowly.

After the fourth day of waiting, strangers began to appear in Carson, a hard-looking, tough bunch of men. They were outlaws and killers and evidently part of the gang. Having heard that Allen was missing, they dared to show their faces. Indeed, they swaggered down the streets of Carson, talking loudly, as though they had nothing further to fear.

"They're in with the gang, all right," Harrison growled to Toothpick as he looked through the windows of the front office of headquarters. "They're comin' out of their holes and gatherin' strength. First thing we know the town'll be infested with 'em just as it was before Jim come to form the Outlaw Legion. Looks like Captain Painton is building his gang up again."

"Yeah, and the worst thing about it is that we can't do nothin' about it till we get proof of it," Toothpick answered. "With Jim gone, they ain't afraid of the rest.

156

There'll be more and more of 'em till we're outnumbered and won't dare to act agin' 'em. Jim would know how to handle 'em, but I don't."

It was not that Toothpick and the others feared the gathering of the gang, but that the loss of Allen had stunned them.

They felt bewildered and helpless. They needed a leader to restore their morale, but there was no one of Allen's courage and energy to take his place. The fact that the gang seemed to be renewing its strength spurred the Rangers to make another search for Allen on the following day.

At noon Toothpick and Doc Candee made a discovery that appalled them and turned them cold as ice. Riding along the bank of the Rio, Toothpick let out a startled shout and raced ahead. At the very edge of the water he jumped out of the saddle and picked something out of the mud.

It was a hat, which he instantly recognized as Allen's. For a while Toothpick and Doc Candee could only stand and stare at it, for it seemed to confirm all their worst fears.

"He's gone. We'll never see him again," Toothpick exclaimed, as he broke down and blubbered like a small boy.

Doc Candee took the hat almost reverently. Tears formed in his eyes as he looked at it. Then the two men turned silently and climbed into their saddles. They started the long ride back to Carson, carrying the heartbreaking news.

It was almost more than they could bear to tell Captain Harrison, Bad Bill Rogers, and the others of the Outlaw Legion of their find. When they finally blurted out their story and displayed the hat, the men who heard it looked stricken.

After the first period of dazed inaction, the Legion strove to organize against the gang which was gathering in the town. Captain Harrison attempted to clear the gang out of Carson by ordering them away, but they only laughed at him. They formed a circle around him and dared him to act.

Harrison knew that if he dared draw a gun to enforce his order, he would be shot down on the spot. The same would happen to the other members of the Legion if they attempted to drive the gang out of Carson. Captain Harrison and his men could only back down and leave them unmolested.

It was the tenth day of Allen's absence when the Legion noticed that the gang was leaving town as quietly as they had come. In twos and threes they mounted their horses and rode away, until none of them remained. Captain Harrison was vastly relieved, but at the same time he suspected the worst.

"They're probably goin' to hold a meetin' somewhere and reorganize," he declared. "And if we tried to fight 'em now we'd be wiped out. They know that Allen's dead and they've taken heart because they've won. Captain Painton will be ownin' the State afore long."

"Yeah, there's nothin' we can do now," Toothpick answered. "We're licked."

By dusk all of the gang had left Carson. In an attempt to discover where the meeting was to be held, some of the Legion followed them. They were fired upon and forced to retreat. Others were warned that another attempt to trail the gang would mean death for the entire Legion.

158

In the face of overwhelming odds, Allen's men were forced to submit. They returned to Carson, more hopeless than ever.

It was next morning that Toothpick was startled almost out of his skin by the discovery of a secret message that had been left for him during the night.

As he crawled out of his bunk, worn from worry, and drew on his boots, he felt something inside one of them. He tried to knock it out, then thrust his hand inside. He found a folded bit of paper. To his astonishment he saw a message scrawled on it and read it:

You and Doc and Bad Bill meet me at sundown near Lost Wagon Gulch. Don't tell no one that you are coming, or that I left you this note.

Jim.

Toothpick stared at the signature as though in a dream. Then he let out a tremendous whoop that shook the walls. It wakened all the others in the building. They came piling out of their bunks demanding to know what had happened.

Toothpick had just time enough to thrust the note into his pocket before they saw it. He told them that he had had a bad dream, and there was nothing to be excited about. But all the time his eyes were dancing joyfully.

Toothpick watched his chance to tell Doc Candee and Bad Bill Rogers of the news.

When they heard his story they were incredulous, but the note convinced them. It was all they could do to contain themselves and keep from shouting the good news at the top of their voices. As best they could, they pretended to be still downcast and morose while they waited for the day to pass.

Then they mounted their horses in a fever of anticipation and rode at top speed toward Lost Wagon Gulch.

The gulch was near the border, and they reached it just as the sun was setting. They stopped and looked around, but there was no sign of Allen. For a few anxious moments they wondered if the note could be a fake; then they saw Allen riding toward them.

Allen was grinning broadly and looked like his old self. King was trotting alongside Princess, swinging his bushy tail. Toothpick, Doc, and Bad Bill howled with joy and raced to meet him. When they swept down upon him, he was lifted bodily from Princess's back and almost crushed in their embraces.

"Gosh, Jim, it's really you," Toothpick blurted.

"Yeah, we'd given you up for lost," Doc Candee cried.

"We thought you was never comin' back," Bad Bill joined in gleefully.

Allen chuckled. "It's me, all right. I sure didn't like to let you think I was dead, but there was nothin' else I could do. I wanted the gang to believe it, so I couldn't tell anybody."

"We found your hat on the bank of the river and thought you'd been killed and throwed in," Toothpick gulped.

"I went into the river and lost my hat, all right," Allen answered in an ominous tone. "I was shot at from behind, and the skunk who did it thought he got me."

"Who was it, Jim?" Candee demanded.

"Dixie Kirk," Allen answered slowly. "He trailed me that night I left Carson. I was close to the edge of the river when he took a shot at me. He didn't even hit me, but I pretended he did, and rolled down the slope into the Rio, I swam under water a little way, then come up under an overhangin' bank, so he couldn't see me."

"I told you he was a killer and shouldn't be trusted," Doc Candee cried. "He might've killed you."

"Yeah, but I'm hard to hit," Allen answered slowly. "I got away, then found Princess runnin' loose, and called for King. He followed my orders and stayed where I sent him. Since then I've been hidin' out, watchin' the gang's operations, and waitin' for our chance to strike at 'em again."

"But you never had any grub. How'd you keep alive, Jim?"

"Gosh, I was taught to rustle a livin' out of the desert when I was a kid," Allen answered sadly. "That wasn't nothin'. The worst of it was lettin' you think I was dead. You never told anybody about my note?"

"Not a soul," Doc Candee declared. "The gang's been comin' into town full force, but now they're gone again. We're sure happy to have you back, for otherwise we couldn't fight 'em any more."

"Yeah, I know what they've been doin'. They've left town to get together across the Rio at the Casa del Diablo," Allen said.

"Captain Painton's place in Mexico?" Bad Bill Rogers asked quickly. "Is Painton there, too?"

"Yeah, I reckon he is," Allen answered softly. "He thinks I'm dead, and he's reorganizin' the gang. Now it's up to us to scatter 'em and get Captain Painton. If we don't do it this time we never will."

What're you plannin' to do, Jim?" Toothpick asked quickly.

"Trap 'em in the Casa," Allen answered flatly. "You three men head back for Carson and get the Legion

161

together again, every man of 'em. Don't leave anybody behind. Wait till after dark, so nobody will know you're leavin'. Then head across the border for the Casa. You know where it is, Toothpick."

"Sure do," Toothpick answered grimly. "But remember the Casa del Diablo is a tough place to try to catch Captain Painton in, Jim," he added anxiously. "When we tried it afore, he got away from us by usin' a secret underground passage connectin' one of the rooms with some place outside of the walls. He might slip out that way again even if we surround the Casa."

"Nope, I know now where that underground passage comes out," Allen answered. "That's one of the things I wanted to find out afore callin' the Legion together, and I did. It was a hard job, but I found tracks that led to it. King helped me find the hole."

"Where is it? We'll see that Captain Painton don't get out that way this time," Doc Candee exclaimed.

Allen wagged his head negatively. "Nope, I'm keepin' that to myself. Gettin' Captain Painton is my personal job, and I'm goin' to do it without any help from anybody else. I'm goin' to use that passage myself. All the rest of you have got to surround the Casa, then break in and round up the gang."

"You mean you won't let any of us help you, Jim?" Toothpick asked with keen disappointment.

"Not any," Jim Allen answered bluntly. "We need all our strength for closin' in on the Casa. You three better be headin' back to Carson now. Be sure and don't tell the Legion what we're goin' to do until the right time comes. Center 'em about the two gates, and when you hear me give my wolf call, rush in. You've got to move fast and take 'em by surprise, otherwise they'll mow you down afore you can get in. The Casa is like a fort,

162

and we'll never take it if you don't act quick.

"If you don't see me anywheres, you'll know I'm busy on my own hook. Don't worry about me. Afterward I'll meet you right in front of the Casa. Wait there for me to show up."

"Where you goin' now, Jim?" Toothpick asked anxiously.

"Back across the border," Allen answered.

"You're takin' a terrible chance, Jim," Toothpick protested. "The gang might spy you, or Lieutenant Casey and his rurales might see you. In either case, you'll be shot on sight."

"I'm not worryin' about that," Allen replied. "It's our last chance to split up the gang. If we fail tonight, we're licked for good. Now start headin' back to Carson, and don't waste any time on the way there."

SHOW-DOWN

THE SKY WAS INKY AS ALLEN RODE SLOWLY THROUGH the hills south of the Rio. Princess moved silently, and King kept close beside her. Both of them seemed to realize that tonight Allen was facing a show-down with the deadliest enemy he had ever met. The wolf dog frequently turned his yellow eyes into Allen's face, and Princess kept on the alert. As they traveled over the crest of a hill, then down into a dark valley, a great quiet surrounded them.

Though another man could have seen nothing, Allen was able to distinguish a structure on the crest of the next hill.

The house looked like several great, square blocks. It was surrounded by a high wall. A road, almost overgrown with range grass, led toward it. It seemed deserted, and there was no apparent indication that it had been used for many years.

He watched it a long while as he stole closer. Then he turned slowly and rode along the slope. The arm of a woods stretched across it, looking like a great black cloud on the ground.

Allen entered the shadows and drifted through the trees silently. At last he came to a stop, looking toward a black hole partly hidden by thick bushes.

This was the end of the underground passageway which connected with the Casa del Diablo. It was so cunningly hidden that its existence would never be suspected by one who had not learned of it. The search for it had cost Allen many hours of arduous effort.

He slipped out of the saddle and inspected the ground. Reassured at what he found—fresh marks indicating that the passage had been used within the last few hours—he remounted Princess.

He went back the way he had come, until he was again within sight of the Casa del Diablo. Then he stopped Princess and sat perfectly still in the saddle. Man and horse seemed like a statue carved from black rock. King, too, was perfectly motionless. The wind was blowing toward Allen, and his keen ears were alert for any sounds carried on it. At last he remarked in a whisper to Princess:

"The Legion's surroundin' the place now, old lady. Hell's goin' to pop in a minute."

Princess twitched her ears nervously, while King whimpered softly. Allen kept looking toward the black hulk of the Casa, waiting. The stealthy sounds, almost inaudible even to his animal-like ears, continued for a few minutes, then finally there was silence.

A long, mournful, shivering sound carried through the night air. It came from Allen's throat—the moan of a lobo wolf. Allen repeated it. For a moment afterward the night was perfectly silent.

Then Allen whirled Princess around and raced toward the entrance of the secret passageway. King bounded along beside him with fangs bared and eyes flaming with yellow.

The air inside the Casa del Diablo was charged with excitement. In the large, bare rooms on the lower floor the members of the gang were gathered. In the candlelight their faces looked more hard and brutal than ever.

The men spoke in hushed tones when they dared speak at all. Sometimes they were quiet and looked toward the stairs which rose to the second floor. They were awaiting Captain Painton's entrance.

On the floor above was a room as barren as the rest of the house. The furniture was plain and heavy, consisting of only a table and two chairs. A tattered curtain hung over the one window opening into it, far above the level of the patio. At the table Captain Painton was sitting, his face shaded by the broad brim of his hat. Standing opposite him was Dixie Kirk, smiling confidently.

"You succeeded in your mission, Kirk, which is more than I can say for any one else who ever tried to kill Allen," Captain Painton said in his harsh tones. "You've received your reward from me, but you failed to get the money on Allen's head because you lost him in the river. Perhaps you feel that you are not sufficiently paid for his death. In that case, you probably will be glad to hear what I'm about to tell you."

Kirk's eyes glistened expectantly.

"Allen succeeded in removing my two chief lieutenants," Captain Painton went on harshly. "First he got Laughing Ed Cummins, then he killed Ed Blendine. I need someone to take their places. You are going to be that man. I trust nobody completely, but you are as reliable as any one else I could expect to find. After this you will take charge of the gang in my absence and see that my orders are carried out to the letter."

"I reckon I can do that, all right, if there's enough in it for me."

Captain Painton's sharklike eyes turned to ice. "You'll be well paid. And you will handle your responsibility as you should, or you will step aside. If—"

He broke off suddenly, then jerked to his feet. Very faintly he heard the long, blood-chilling wolf call as it penetrated the walls. Dixie Kirk also heard it, and his face went pale. Captain Painton whipped around and faced Kirk, making a move to draw his Colts.

"That's Allen's signal," Painton gasped.

"No, it's nothin' but a wolf out in the hills," Kirk exclaimed in terror.

"It's a human wolf; it's Allen," Painton snapped.

"It can't be Allen. Allen's dead. You saw him yourself when he fell into the river. You was lookin' out of the cabin and satisfied yourself that—"

"Then he's got more than one life, because he's outside now," Painton interrupted him wrathfully. "Kirk, you've failed like all the others. I promised you you'd pay for that."

He jerked out his gun. For an instant Dixie Kirk was terrified. He felt that death was near. He knew that if he dared attempt to shoot Captain Painton, the men downstairs would kill him before he could leave the Casa. Therefore, he made no move to draw his gun. As

166

Captain Painton's weapon came up, he cried:

"You can't be sure it's Allen. And even if it is, it don't matter. You've got your men here and he can't touch you."

Captain Painton stood rigid, pointing the gun at Kirk's chest. Kirk expected a bullet to crash into his body at any instant. Then Painton's eyes gleamed anew.

"You're right; Allen will never get me. Let him come and try it, if he's out there. The gang will kill every one of his men if they—"

Again he broke off, startled into speechlessness. From outside came the clatter of hoofs. Shrill cries followed, then the horses rushed across the patio. Guns began to explode. From the floor below came hoarse shouts, and the sound of men stampeding through the Casa.

"They're on us already!" Captain Painton shouted.

Painton had not expected an attack so soon. He turned from Dixie Kirk, seeming to forget his threats against Kirk's life. Hastily he crossed the room and jerked aside the curtain of the window. Looking down into the patio, he saw the Legion riders circling the Casa, a firing and shouting whirlwind. Then he whirled back, stopped at the table, and grasped its edge.

He commanded Kirk to place the oil lamp on the floor. As Kirk did this, Captain Painton tilted the table. When it moved, a section of the floor on which it had been standing came up with it. A dark space yawned below, and a flight of stairs could be seen leading up to the level of the floor. Painton curtly commanded Kirk to descend. Kirk quickly complied, then the captain followed, carrying the lamp.

They were in a secret room which could not be

reached in any other way. It had no windows and no door. Dixie Kirk did not realize that no other member of the gang had ever entered this room. Captain Painton had kept its existence a secret and had used it himself as his headquarters. Only this unforeseen extremity could have forced him to reveal it to another man.

Painton placed the lamp on a table, then crossed the room swiftly, toward a cupboard against the wall. He swung open the double doors, and as he did so a gust of cold, damp air came out of them and made the lamp flicker. Painton stood aside and snarled at Kirk.

"Go in first. This tunnel takes us outside the Casa. We'll wait for Allen to show up. When he does, we'll get him together."

"I tell you Allen's dead."

"Don't argue; get into the tunnel," Painton roared.

Kirk obeyed. He had to stoop to pass through the doors of the cupboard. Ahead of him he saw only earthen walls stretching away into darkness. He stumbled through, then found himself in a passageway large enough to permit him to stand upright. Turning, he watched Captain Painton scramble in after him.

The noise of the fighting penetrated into the secret room. The house was full of screaming, cursing men, and guns were blasting constantly. Above the uproar could be heard the blood-chilling battle cry of the Outlaw Legion:

"Come on, wolves!"

Then the swinging cupboard doors closed, and thick darkness enwrapped the underground passage. Dixie Kirk groped through the blackness, feeling the damp walls as he progressed, while Captain Painton followed at his heels.

Immediately after uttering his wolf call, Jim-twin Allen rushed across the slope toward the end of the secret tunnel. He slipped off Princess's back and huddled for a moment, listening. King stood beside him silently. Then Allen rose, parted the bushes, and ducked through them. King kept close, his yellow eyes flaring.

Allen passed along the tunnel without a sound. It was so black that even his keen eyesight was useless. Not the slightest ray of light showed him what lay ahead. He did not know how long the passage was or what pitfalls lay in his path.

He groped on, feeling King brush against him now and then. There was no sound but the wolf dog's rapid breathing.

Suddenly Allen stopped. He sensed a movement ahead, then heard a voice. It was the harsh tones of Captain Painton. King stopped beside Allen and stood motionless. Allen's muscles tightened as he waited.

The sounds in the tunnel continued and grew louder. He could distinguish that two men were moving toward him. He deliberately waited as they came closer. Without warning a low, threatening growl came from King's throat.

Instantly the sounds of movement stopped. The voice of Dixie Kirk came out of the blackness as he gasped:

"What was that?"

"Fool, use your gun!" Captain Painton bellowed.

The voices rang hollowly along the tunnel. Allen crouched down and shouted:

"Hang on your ears!"

His answer was a shot from Dixie Kirk's six-gun. The explosion was ear-splitting in the confined space. The flash of light was blinding. It lasted only a split second, but it enabled Allen to see Kirk crouching against the side of the passage, and Captain Painton huddling beyond. The bullet whizzed past Allen's head and slapped into the damp earth of the wall.

A savage snarl came from King's throat. He leaped with the quickness of lightning. A shrill cry of terror answered his attack. Then for a moment there was the sound of a desperate struggle. Dixie Kirk screamed again, and King's snarls became more ferocious.

Allen groped forward, trying to force his way past the struggling forms, but he could not. Then King gave a louder growl, and a sputtering sound followed. A deep silence ensued.

Allen half expected an attack from Captain Painton, but none came. He quickly slipped a match from his pocket and struck it. Its light gleamed along the dark passageway, but Captain Painton was not in sight.

Almost at Allen's feet Dixie Kirk lay dead in a pool of blood. King stood over him, yellow eyes flaring savagely. His sharp fangs had ripped Kirk's throat. Allen's face was merciless as he stepped across Kirk's body.

"Stay back, King," he called.

He knew that Captain Painton had retreated during the confusion of King's attack on Dixie Kirk. Thinking that Painton might escape through a branch tunnel, he ran deeper into the tunnel. Suddenly he collided with something that stopped him short. Reaching forward, he found that the tunnel terminated abruptly, except for a square hole in the wall.

Quickly he struck another match and looked into the interior of the cupboard. He realized that Captain Painton was beyond the two small doors and that when he passed through them he would be at a tremendous disadvantage. He raised his two Colts, crawled into the hole, then poised for the rush that would send him through the doors into the room beyond.

When he leaped, the doors flew open and he bounded into the room. Instantly he sprang aside, ready for an attack. Captain Painton was standing on the other side of the room, facing him.

Painton was holding the oil lamp in one hand, from which he had removed the chimney. In the other he was gripping a six-shooter, though he made no move to use it. At his feet a small trapdoor was raised, disclosing a black, open space below. When Allen saw that Painton was not going to fire, he straightened grimly and lowered his guns.

"We meet again, Allen, for the last time," Captain Painton declared.

"I reckon it is for the last time," Allen declared in a hard, cold voice.

He studied Captain Painton, whose eyes were glittering like frost. His thin lips were curled into a contemptuous, evil smile. Desperation and a grim intention were pictured on his face.

"You never kept your part of the bargain," Allen declared after a moment of silence. "When you thought I was killed, you reckoned you didn't have anything more to fear. Now I'm here to make you settle for not heedin' my warnin'."

Captain Painton snarled. "I was a fool to listen to you, Allen. You bluffed me, that's all. You took me by surprise, and I didn't realize it at the time. You don't know who I am, and you never will."

Allen's wolfish eyes glinted hard as he answered. "I wasn't bluffin' you. I was tellin' the truth. I was makin' you a bargain so's I wouldn't have to kill you. Now

171

you're forcin' me to do what I never wanted to do."

"You can't frighten me, Allen," Captain Painton snapped. "Your bluff won't work."

"I learned who you was the day you stopped Mrs. Stringer's hosses from runnin' away," Allen answered flatly. "You gave yourself away doin' that. I trailed you to your hideaway on the Rio by slippin' out to the stable one night and filin' a nick in the frog of one of your hoss's hoofs. That made an easy trail to follow. Since that day in Carson there ain't been any doubt in my mind who you are."

Captain Painton stared fixedly. "I don't believe that you wouldn't expose me if you got the chance. You'd do it, and gloat over it the rest of your days."

"I gave you my word I'd never tell anybody, and I'm goin' to keep that promise if it's humanly possible," Allen answered. "I'd rather die myself than let your family know the side of you that you've kept from 'em."

"I don't believe you, Allen," Captain Painton declared raspingly. "But that doesn't matter. You're never going to have a chance to tell any one who I really am. You're never going to leave this room alive."

They gazed at each other a full minute. From outside the Casa, and from the other rooms in the house, came the continual noise of fighting. Again and again the rallying cry of the Outlaw Legion sounded triumphantly. Both Captain Painton and Allen realized that the Legion had gained the advantage in the battle.

Painton sneered. "Allen, I know that the game is up as far as I'm concerned, and I'm ready to go. But when I do, you'll die with me, and all of the men in this house will be blown to bits."

Allen's strange, slanted eyes narrowed. "I reckon you

ain't scarin' me any," he said flatly. "Bluffin' won't work now."

"You'll soon find out that I'm speakin' the truth," Captain Painton declared rapidly, and his eyes flared with the wild light of a maniac. "You see this trapdoor open at my feet? Beneath it are a dozen open kegs of gunpowder. Packed around them are scores of boxes of dynamite. There is enough to blow the Casa to atoms, along with everything inside it. I'm holding this lamp in my hand, ready to drop it. When I do, it will all be over in a second. You and me and every man inside the Casa will die."

Allen raised his guns. He commanded flatly: "Back away from that hole. Do it quick, or I'll drop you."

Captain Painton laughed insanely. "I have nothing to fear from you, Allen. Shoot if you like. When the bullet hits me I will drop the lamp. In fact, I invite you to shoot. It will hasten the end."

For a moment Allen was at a loss. He realized that he could not force Captain Painton back from the yawning trapdoor. He knew that to shoot would indeed bring about the instant destruction of the Casa. Captain Painton laughed again, in confident triumph, at Allen's look of defeat.

Even if Allen shot at the lamp, and broke it, the danger would remain. In fact, the flying oil would ignite from the wick and the explosion of the powder cached below the room would be all the more certain.

Though Allen could shoot with absolute accuracy, he did not dare try to extinguish the broad wick with a bullet. He was too likely to fail to put it out with one slug, and failure would mean the death of his Legion.

He looked down at the black hole in the floor. The

cover of it was standing upright, held by its hinges. Beneath was darkness, except for the glow of the lamp which filtered through. By means of it Allen could see the boxes of dynamite stacked below. He slowly lowered his guns, a look of supreme resignation on his face.

"I reckon you've got me licked," he said slowly.

Painton uttered a cackling laugh. "At last the great Jim-twin Allen is through," he gloated. "At last he's come to the end of his string. I've proven too much for him."

It was during the very moment of Captain Painton's keenest triumph, when he raised his head and laughed, that he permitted himself to lower his guard.

For a second his eyes were taken from Allen, and during that second, Allen acted. He leaped forward swiftly and kicked out. The toe of his boot struck the raised trapdoor with sudden force.

At the same instant Captain Painton recovered. With an oath he flung the lamp downward. It struck the trapdoor just as the section of flooring dropped into place. The lamp did not break, but rolled across the boards. Allen leaped up suddenly, standing on the trapdoor, and pushed Captain Painton aside. Painton bellowed with wrath and reached for his gun.

Allen did not make a move toward his Colts. Captain Painton paused, backed to the wall, his eyes flaring with madness. Allen faced him squarely.

"We're fightin' it to a finish now. I'm givin' you a chance like every other man I ever faced. I'm countin' three," he declared softly.

Painton stared. His hand moved slowly toward his gun, while Allen's hung motionless.

"One," Allen counted.

Captain Painton's hand moved more quickly. He gripped his Colt but did not lift it. His muscles tensed for a lightning draw. Allen's yellow-flecked eyes fastened on him.

"Two."

A scream came from Captain Painton's throat as he jumped aside and drew. He fired twice in swift succession. The bullets sped past Allen as he jumped away. Again Captain Painton fired, in a desperate frenzy, while Allen bounded about. And then Allen made his draw. He fell into a crouch and pulled the triggers of his guns.

Captain Painton fell against the wall. He clutched at his chest and throat as he slid downward. When he struck the floor he rolled over and lay still. Allen stared at him with merciless eyes as savage as the eyes of a wolf. Then he stepped close, with slow, deliberate movements. With a jerk he ripped the false beard from the dead man's face.

With its removal, Captain Painton's features seemed to change. The transformation was so complete and sudden that even Allen, who knew what the result would be, was astounded.

The man who had died was Amos Stringer!

THE LONG TRAIL CALLS

ALLEN LOOKED HOPELESSLY SAD AS HE GAZED DOWN at Stringer's body. A great sigh came from his lungs and he said aloud:

"I never wanted to do it, but you forced me to. It was either you or my men."

For a long while Allen stood there looking at the man

175

who had been Captain Painton. All around the Casa the noise of the battle continued, though it was diminishing. Allen turned away slowly. He replaced the smoking lamp on the table, then stood motionless, thinking rapidly.

At last he moved toward the cupboard doors and opened them. He came back, stooped, and lifted Stringer's body in his arms. Though Stringer was large and heavy, Allen carried him without apparent effort. He took Stringer through the opening into the tunnel, then shut the doors behind him. Tottering through the dark tunnel he went on, slowly, carrying his grim burden.

The Outlaw Legion was gathered in the patio of the Casa del Diablo when Allen rode through the gate. His appearance was greeted with shouts and cheers. He looked exhausted and sad in spite of the fact that the Legion had succeeded in its objective.

"Jim, there ain't any more gang," Toothpick Jarrick sang out jubilantly. "Half of 'em are dead and we've got the other half prisoners. We sure wolfed 'em this time."

"Good, but did we lose any men?" Allen asked quickly.

"Yeah, Pat Garrett got it," Doc Candee said solemnly. "I was with him when he died, and he was askin' for you. He said he hoped the White Wolf never stopped ridin'."

Allen's throat grew tight. He turned away to cover his grief, and quickly issued orders.

"Tie up the prisoners and start 'em back to Carson. I've got to be hurryin' ahead, so Lieutenant Casey and his rurales won't see me. Keep the prisoners together as best you can, and be in town by sunup."

"All right, Jim, but what've you been doin'?" Toothpick demanded. "What about Captain Painton?"

"He's dead," Allen said slowly.

"Dead? Then you got him! He won't ever run any more dope," Bad Bill Rogers whooped.

"Who was he, Jim? Did you find out?" Toothpick demanded.

To remain true to his promise, Allen was forced to lie. "He wasn't anybody I ever saw afore," he said. "He slipped out the secret passage, and I chased him to the Rio. I got him when he was gettin' across, and he fell into the river. I reckon nobody'll ever see him again."

"Yeah, but are you sure he was Captain Painton?" Doc Candee asked excitedly.

Allen removed the false beard from his pocket. "He was puttin' this on when I surprised him in a secret room at the end of the tunnel, and dropped it. You better take it. I don't ever want to see it again."

He tossed the thing away at random and did not look to see who caught it. Then he turned Princess away.

"Where you goin', Jim?" Toothpick demanded.

"I've got an important message to take. I'll see you all in Carson tomorrow mornin'," Allen answered quickly, and he rode off.

An hour past sunup Allen rode through the gate of the Circle G. Jeff Gordon saw him jogging toward the house and hurried to meet him. Already the news had come from Carson that Allen was alive. The Outlaw Legion had returned, and every one knew that the gang was at last broken up. Jeff Gordon rained congratulations on Allen. Mrs. Stringer and Nora came out of the house, and when Allen saw them he felt a flash of keen pain.

He went onto the porch, and Mrs. Stringer clasped him in her arms. She sobbed and laughed at the same time. Nora impulsively kissed Allen and chattered at him happily. Allen's face remained sad and wistful, and at last they asked him what was the matter. The moment had come when he must tell them. He looked straight into Mrs. Stringer's eyes and began.

"We wiped out the gang, but we paid a terrible price to do it, he said slowly. "You never knew it, but Amos Stringer was helpin' me."

"But Amos said he was goin' back to Birchill when he left yesterday," Jeff Gordon boomed. "He never said he knew you was alive or that he was goin' to help you, Jim."

"He kept it secret because I asked him to," Allen answered.

Suddenly Mrs. Stringer asked with a catch in her voice: "Jim Allen, what has happened to Amos?"

"Amos fought right beside me, Mrs. Stringer," Allen lied gallantly. "He was wounded bad, but he kept right on fightin'. Afore it was all over, he was gone. There wasn't nothin' I could do but bury him where he fell. He's over by a clump of trees near Twin Peak, across the border."

Mrs. Stringer grew pale. Nora's eyes became filled with tears as she put her arms around her mother. For a moment Jeff Gordon was prepared to see his sister break down with grief, but Mrs. Stringer raised her chin resolutely and kept her eyes dry.

"I'm proud that Amos died by your side, Jim Allen. He was a fine man, and it was a fitting end."

Then she could say no more. She sank into a chair and cried silently. Nora kept a firm grip on herself and Jeff Gordon took her in his huge arms. They were so overcome by the news of their bereavement that they did not see Allen turning sadly away. But when they looked up he was gone.

Allen had kept his promise. The secret was his alone, and it would go with him to his grave.

Allen, with Toothpick Jarrick and Kip Jerome, slipped into Carson without any one seeing them. There was clamor in the streets; ranchers and cowhands for miles around were trooping into the town to hear the news at firsthand.

The bars were doing a rushing business, celebrating half the time by dispensing drinks free. The Rangers and the Outlaw Legion were proclaimed everywhere as heroes, and Jim Allen's name was shouted frequently by men who wanted to see him and congratulate him for exterminating the last of the dreaded gang. But Allen turned a deaf ear and kept quietly out of sight.

He went into the space behind the headquarters and harnessed his horse. Then he slipped into the rear office, which was empty, and gathered his belongings. In a few minutes his pack was loaded. After that Allen went inside again. In a few minutes he walked into the front office.

Governor Harrison was there, and saw him first. The governor rushed at him and clasped his hand and began booming out his praises. The others crowded around him. Then Captain Harrison noticed that Allen had changed clothes.

"Where's your uniform, Jim?" he asked.

"I left it back in my office," Allen answered slowly. "I won't ever wear it again. I'm resignin'."

"Resignin'?" the crowd chorused.

For a moment they were stunned into silence, then the clamor began again. To all their entreaties Allen made no answer. In his patched flannel shirt, overalls, and high-topped moccasins, he was a forlorn figure. Finally the bunch around him ran out of breath, and Allen grasped the opportunity to say to Toothpick:

"Call the Legion together out in front, Toothpick. I want to say somethin' to them."

As Toothpick rushed off, Governor Harrison grasped Allen's arm.

"Look here, Jim, there's no need of your resigning," he boomed. "You're the best officer this State has got, not barring even my brother. He'd join me in what I say. We mustn't lose you. Harry ain't goin' to stay in the service much longer, and when he resigns I'll make you chief of all the Rangers in the State."

"Shucks, that's sure kind of you, but I reckon I wasn't cut out to be a law officer all my life," Allen answered slowly. "I've been ridin' the long trail so long that I reckon I can never do anything else."

"But, Jim, you've got to stay here a while anyway," Captain Harrison exclaimed. "You're free on bail, you know, and we've got to go through a few formalities before the governor can issue you a pardon. You've got to be brought to trial. There ain't a jury that wouldn't acquit you. Then you could make your home here in the State and live in peace."

"Shucks, there'll never be any peace for me," Allen answered wistfully. "I'm an outlaw and folks could never forget that. Besides, I couldn't stay tied down to one place. I ain't happy unless I'm wanderin'."

"You mean you won't stay? I can't issue you a pardon unless you do," Governor Harrison protested.

"I don't want the pardon," Allen answered. "It's nothin' but a piece of paper. I'm a wolf, and a pardon won't make me anything different. Nope, I'm leavin' right away. My hosses is ready to go, and so am I."

In the yard in front of the Ranger headquarters Allen's men had come together. There were few of them now, not nearly so many as when he had organized the Outlaw Legion. Most of their number had died fighting the gang. Allen looked into their faces, and his eyes grew even sadder than before.

"You men have stood by me, and I owe you more'n I can say," he began simply. "You come because I asked you to, and risked your lives. Folks may call you outlaws and killers, and the law may be huntin' you in other States, but you're my friends. If most men was as fearless and loyal as you have been, it would be a better world to live in. Now our job is done, and I've got to say 'so long' to you."

They were silent as he paused. Toothpick Jarrick stood near Allen, and with him was Doc Candee and Bad Bill Rogers. They were the three who had been closest to him. He looked at them and smiled slowly.

"You helped me form the Legion, and now I reckon you'll help me disband it. I'm leavin' it all in your hands. There's no use of me tryin' to thank you for what you done, you know how I feel about it. You know that if you need me, I'll come."

"Gosh, we're goin' along with you," Toothpick Jarrick choked.

"Nope, I'm goin' off alone," Allen answered.

"Jim, we're sure goin' to miss you," Doc Candee said.

"Yeah, and we'll always wear our wolf pins to remember the time when we fought the gang with you," Bad Bill Rogers exclaimed.

Then they pressed forward and grasped his hand. They did not speak, for words were beyond them. When they turned away, Allen stepped back into the door. He looked around and called:

"So long, wolves."

"So long, Jim!"

Captain Harry Harrison grasped Allen's hands fervently and tried to express his thanks, but he only mumbled. The grizzled old Ranger was too overcome. Then the regular Rangers crowded around Allen. Governor Harrison tried again to implore him to stay, but it was useless.

At last, when he saw his chance, Allen slipped out the rear door of the building and rode away.

On Princess's back, with his pack horse trailing behind, and King trotting alongside, he rode out of Carson.

One by one the old members of the Outlaw Legion mounted their horses and silently left Carson.

By dark all of them were gone, the wolf pack was scattered.

And somewhere out in the Barrens, Jim-twin Allen, a hunted outlaw again, was riding the endless trail—alone.